Free to Kill
A Katie Freeman Mystery

By Julie Mellon

ISBN: 978-1503209015 (print)
ISBN: 978-0-9862997-0-4 (ebook)

Dedication

To my mom, who always believed in me.

A Word from the Author

There are so many people that have helped make this dream come true for me. Once I voiced this dream, the encouragement came from all sides. So, I would like to say a special thank you to those that have had a hand in the completion of this book. First, to my beta readers, Michelle Bukowski, Sarah Ross and Laura Haines, without your feedback, Katie and her crew would be a lot more disorganized. Thank you for the comments, corrections, and what-were-you-thinking (?!?!) responses you gave. I love how you all began to wonder about my sanity when I would get excited talking about medieval torture!

Second, to Ryan Bukowski. I love your creative genius when it comes to photography and meshing different elements together. You and Michelle dreamed up a fantastic cover for me, and you brought it to life with great skill. I look forward to seeing what you come up with in the future.

To Mike Spring, thank you for your editing genius. Without your help, my book would be incomplete. Thanks for your patience as I questioned your changes and for not being afraid to tell me your thoughts.

Finally, to Michelle Bukowski, I don't know how I would have done this journey without you. You have been invaluable: from your photography skills, to your web designs, to your creativity. My social media and online presence wouldn't be what it is today without your dedicated effort. You have pushed me out of my comfort zone on more than one occasion during this process, for which I will be forever grateful. Thank you!

Table of Contents

Prologue

Charlene moved through the house as quietly as her abused body would allow. She hadn't been able to stand upright in nearly two weeks thanks to the two broken ribs courtesy of her husband. But those two broken ribs had given her a new lease on life. Charlene would never forget the minute when the nurse looked up and said those magic words: you're pregnant. Even though the nurse's disgusted look spoke volumes, Charlene's heart soared; then the terror set in. Charlene might not have the courage to stand against her husband for herself, but she knew she could do it to protect her unborn daughter. She didn't know why she knew it was a girl, but she did.

Tonight was the weekly lottery drawing. Hank never missed watching it and waiting for the time when his numbers would be chosen. It was a must see event in the Stephens household, and also one of the most terrifying. Two weeks before, Hank had been just drunk enough to be mean when the numbers called weren't his. Hank had levels of mean: just buzzed would mellow him out; still functional but drunk would make him strike out; slurred drunk would make him maudlin; and just plain old drunk would make him pass out. Charlene had learned to time the beers so that he was only buzzed or slurred drunk when the numbers were read. If he was still functional, she knew her evening would end with a trip to the emergency room. And she knew the doctors and nurses were tired of seeing her come in.

They no longer even bothered to ask what happened or to call the police when she arrived. They just patched her up and sent her on her way with a new supply of pain medicine. One thing Charlene had learned to handle was pain. Because of this, she also had an impressive stash of heavy-duty painkillers.

Two weeks ago, Hank had come home early while Charlene had still been at the grocery store. When she got home, Hank had already started on the Budweiser - that was never a good sign. She had hurried to get dinner fixed, hoping that some food would counteract the booze before it got out of hand. Luck had not been with her that night, and Hank was still functional when the numbers were read. Charlene ended up in the hospital and left with another prescription for painkillers and the knowledge that she was pregnant.

She waited a few days for the bruising on her face to go away. Then she went to get money. Charlene had never been one to go about life by breaking the rules, but she knew now that her only hope was to do something she would never think of doing on a normal day. Growing up, she prayed that her mom would leave her dad and take them away. Then she ended up marrying a man just like her dad and realized how easy it was to become her mother. She was determined that her daughter would know a different life.

Charlene's cousin Billy knew how to get money for the pills she had stashed. She only took thirty pills with her, hoping that would be enough. Billy also knew people who could help with other things Charlene would need. He had offered to help her get away from Hank several times, but Charlene always turned him down.

When Billy saw Charlene on his porch, he opened the screen, "Well, don't you look worse for the wear." His eyes were kind, but the last thing Charlene needed was sympathy. She had to remain strong.

"I need money, Billy, and a new identity." Charlene didn't make eye contact; she just stared at the floor. When Billy didn't answer, she glanced up to see him frowning down at her. "Please don't judge me. I just want to get away. You know divorcing him won't help me none. He can still get me if he knows where I am. I just gotta get outta here. I brought these. Thought you might help me sell them and get some money." Charlene held out the sandwich bag with the thirty pills inside.

Billy let out a long low whistle. "What are you doing with Oxy?"

"The hospital's been givin' it to me for all the times I been visitin'. Can you help me?"

"These will get you $50 a pill, so about $1,500. I can have the money by Monday. I got a big need for these. If you got anymore, you let me know." Billy took the bag and walked into the kitchen. Charlene slowly followed him into the next room.

"How quick could you get me more money, if I were to have more pills?" That was more money than she had ever had and more than she expected to get from the pills. She had at least sixty more pills at home and the new prescription for another thirty. Ninety more pills! That was a whole lot of money. It was enough to get her far, far away from LaVergne,

Tennessee. "And what about my other problem? I gotta get outta here, Billy."

Billy stared her down for a few minutes, and then he picked up his phone and made a call. "My cousin needs your assistance. Can you come to my place?" A few head nods and grunts later, Billy hung up the phone. "Can you hang around for a few minutes?" Though it wasn't a question, exactly, Charlene knew he wouldn't have stopped her if she walked out the door. Instead, she simply sat back in the chair and accepted the glass of iced tea Billy handed her.

Neither of them spoke as they waited for Billy's guest to arrive. Charlene could see the questions in Billy's eyes when she glanced up at him, but she didn't have the strength to voice all the horrors Hank had put her through. She also knew that if Billy knew everything, Hank wouldn't stand a chance of walking again, possibly of breathing again. The last thing Charlene wanted was to be shackled to a cripple, and she knew she could never leave him if he was injured. She also knew she couldn't live under the suspicion if he just disappeared. No, the best thing for all concerned was if she just quietly walked away.

Ten minutes passed before there was a knock at the door. Billy got up and went to let in his associate. Victor was a very small man in his mid- to late 50s. He walked in, shook Charlene's hand and sat down at the table. "I will make what you need for $500. That is a deal, only because you are related to Billy. Now, what do you need?"

Charlene was taken aback for a second. "Well, I need to disappear. To have no one looking for me and no one to know who I am or my new name."

"Have you picked a name?"

All at once, Charlene knew what she wanted her name to be. She hadn't even thought that far before asking Billy for help but, for some reason, she knew what her new name had to be. "Yes," she answered.

"Don't say it; just write it down and sign that name below it." Victor slid a tablet of paper across the table. Charlene picked it up and did as he told her. Billy hadn't said a word; he just looked on with his arms crossed as he leaned against the cabinet. "Now, just let me get a few headshots of you, and I will be on my way." Victor pulled out a camera from his bag and took a few close up pictures. He put the equipment away along with the note pad. "I will have your documents ready Monday. You will have the money. We will meet here at 6:00 pm." He picked up his bag and walked out the door.

As the screen slammed behind him, Charlene let out a breath she didn't know she had been holding. Standing up, she walked over and gave Billy a hug. "Thank you for helping me." Then she too walked out the door and hurried home before Hank got there.

The three days until Monday were interminably long. Charlene tried to keep herself busy. Her house was spotless, all the laundry was done, the floors had been scrubbed to the point you could eat off of them, and all the errands were finished early. But finally, Monday arrived. Charlene went to Billy's early so she could get her money and also to take him all the additional pills she had. She had filled the most recent prescription and had eighty-eight pills in her bag this time.

When she handed them to Billy, his eyes bugged out and he nearly fainted. "What the hell, Char? Why you got so many pills? And why have you just been keepin' them? You shoulda brought them to me sooner."

"I didn't need money sooner, or I woulda brought 'em to you then. I need money now. Can you get me money for 'em same as you got for them others?" The thought of selling them on the street made her sick. She knew the trouble these would cause, but she also understood that her needs had to come first for once.

Billy waved her to a seat in the dining room and went upstairs. Charlene listened as first the stairs and then the hallway floorboards creaked under Billy's feet. The house was in terrible shape, and she was so nervous that she was tempted to get up and start cleaning the mound of dishes in his sink. Before she could do just that, Billy reappeared.

"Didn't know you would be bringing me so many. I got enough to cover the whole cost, but it will damn near wipe me out."

"You will get your money back when you sell them, right?" Charlene's concern for her cousin was obvious.

"Don't you worry none 'bout me. I ain't gonna cheat you or me. Now you just put that away before Victor gets here. Keep out what you need to pay him, but nothin' else. He might know me, but he is out for hisself. You gonna tell me what name you done picked?"

"I can't Billy, but I promise, I will let you know that I'm okay." Though Charlene hadn't thought twice about leaving the rest of her family, she would really miss Billy. He had always been there for her. He always made sure she was bandaged up as a kid and that no one in school picked on her. Charlene had been smart in school, but she was also beautiful. It was that beauty that always brought the wrong attention. She blamed her beauty for making her marry Hank. If she had just been a nerdy girl, she would have gone to college. But she had been desperate to escape her father, so when Hank became interested in her, she turned to marriage instead.

The screen door opening jarred her out of her thoughts. Charlene looked up as Victor walked into the room. Tonight, he carried only a small folder. As he sat down, he slid the folder across the table to her. Charlene opened it and looked at a new birth certificate, social security card and driver's license. Her face looked up at her from the new license, startling her with the gaunt appearance. Her new signature was at the bottom. After looking through them, she slid the money across the table. Victor picked it up, and without counting it, turned and walked out of the house. The entire transaction had taken under five minutes and not a word had been spoken. Charlene felt the weight lift from her shoulders for the first time in a long while. Just having the documents and the money were enough to allow her to taste the freedom coming her way.

Two nights later, Charlene stood in the kitchen, barely moving and aching to stand up straight. Tonight was drawing night. Hank would be home in a few minutes and would be ready for food and a beer. Moving carefully, Charlene took two pills from her pocket. She had kept these from Billy just so she could help ease Hank into passing out. That was the only way she was going to get out of the house and away from town. She carefully mashed the pills into a powder and mixed them into his mashed potatoes. As Hank walked through the door, she cut him a piece of meatloaf and added it to the plate, then covered everything with gravy. Hank sat down at the table, took a long drink of his first beer and dug into the food on his plate. He never said a word. When he was done he got up, leaving his plate and empty can on the table and made his way to the recliner in the living room. "Woman, bring me another beer." The bellow was the first he spoke since walking into the house. He lifted the footrest of the recliner and turned on the TV. Charlene handed him the beer and went to clean the kitchen. Her hands were shaking as she wiped the stove and counters. Every fifteen minutes, she took Hank another beer.

By the time the 10:00pm news came on, Hank was well past functional drunk. His head kept falling to the side, waking him with a jerk. At 10:55 his head fell to the side and he let out a loud snore, but never woke back up. Charlene tiptoed down the hall and grabbed the suitcase she had hidden under the bed. She had packed away all the clothes that he wouldn't notice missing had he gone into the closet. Now she hurried and threw all the rest of her clothes into the suitcase. She grabbed the folder with her new identity from under the spare room mattress, grabbed her purse and headed back down the hall as quietly as she could. Just as she got to the living room, the announcer on T.V. began announcing the lottery numbers. At the first number, she paused to listen. Hank always played the same numbers: 6-19-28-35-48 and a Powerball of 15. In stunned silence, she listened as one after another of the numbers matched.

Two minutes after the numbers were read, the ringing of the phone shocked her out of her stupor. Holy cow! They had won the lottery! Quickly turning the ringer off so the phone wouldn't wake Hank, Charlene reached over and picked up the ticket from the end table. Without so much as one final look over her shoulder, she turned and walked out the door.

Twenty-six years later

Chapter One

Katie nervously smoothed her hand over her dark hair, making sure each strand was in place. She tugged her navy blazer down over her matching skirt. Today was her first day at her new job. Though she had been with the FBI for three years, she had only recently accepted a transfer to the Tennessee office. Taking a deep breath, she pushed open the door and walked into the three-story building that looked like a giant bar code you would find on a product label. The windows were straight columns with the shades in various offices adjusted to different heights. This would be her new workplace for the foreseeable future.

Approaching the front desk, Katie pulled out her credentials to display to the security guard at the front counter. The guard took her identification without looking up from the monitor he was watching, his bald head reflecting the glare of the florescent lights. His head jerked up, eyebrows raised to what was once his hairline, as he glanced from her photo to her face. Katie was getting used to this reaction from men, though it still puzzled her. She knew her waist length hair was something to gawk at, but her hair was in a tightly woven bun, both in the photo and in person. Standing at 5'9", she was not exceptionally tall, and with brown hair and bright green eyes, she considered herself average looking. But since leaving her sheltered home seven years ago for college, she had experienced this reaction from several men. She had been told more than once that she looked exotic. To her that was just a polite way of saying "different" and she didn't want to be different. She wanted to blend in.

Choosing to ignore the reaction, she said in a clipped tone, "I'm new to the office. Can you tell me where I can find Special Agent in Charge Nelson?"

"Um, he's on the third floor, room 311. Just take the elevator and turn right. It's at the end of the hall," the guard replied

Katie had a fear of elevators, but not wanting to admit that to a complete stranger, she asked if there were stairs available. The guard handed back her credentials and pointed to a door to the right of the elevator. Nodding her thanks, Katie turned and headed in the direction he indicated.

Once on the third floor, she closed her eyes and took a few deep breaths to calm her nerves before opening the door to the hallway. When she opened her eyes, there was a man holding the door open, as if he were attempting to go downstairs. He was, quite simply...stunning. Wearing a charcoal gray suit and royal purple shirt topped off with a lavender tie, his brown eyes were as warm as liquid chocolate. "Excuse me," the man said, "can I help you find where you're going?" There was no mistaking the interest in his eyes as they passed from her head to her toes and back.

"No, thank you. I was just catching my breath." Katie brushed past him and into the hall, not knowing if her irritation was from his perusal or her own reaction to the stranger. Choosing to believe it was because he had blatantly checked her out was easier than admitting she was attracted to him. Didn't the men in this building see women every day? She wasn't something to be stared at, just because she was in the vicinity. With that thought in her head, she made her way to the end of the hall as directed. Luckily the person sitting behind the desk in front of room 311 was a woman. A very pregnant woman; so pregnant that Katie worried that one move would send her into labor. Did women really work that close to delivery? Shaking the thought out of her head, Katie cleared her throat and prepared to present her credentials to the woman.

The woman looked up and smiled. "It won't be necessary to pull those out. I've been expecting you. Al called up from the desk to let me know you were on you way. Have a seat and I will let Marty - I mean SAC Nelson - know you're here. Nick - I mean ASAC Perry - will be joinin' you." The woman's voice was sugary sweet and her drawl took some getting used to in order to figure out what she was saying. Katie simply smiled and nodded, wanting to offer assistance as the woman heaved her body out of the chair. "Oh, by the way, I'm Jessie. Jessie Glenn." With that, she lumbered into room 311 to announce Katie's arrival.

Katie could hear the mumble of voices coming from the office and a few seconds later Jessie reemerged and lowered herself back into her chair. Her face was red and she was breathing heavily from even that small amount of exertion. Jessie reached for the phone, dialed a few numbers, and announced Katie's arrival, presumably to 'Nick, I mean ASAC Perry'. Katie nearly smiled at the thoughts running through her head, but the groan from Jessie had her looking up in alarm. Jessie sat back and rubbed her extremely distended stomach. "I sure will be glad when this little feller arrives. I am so tired of him dancin' on my guts." Continuing as if nothing had been said, Jessie again picked up the phone and dialed a few numbers. She announced Katie's arrival to yet another person before returning the phone to the cradle. "Your new partner, Michael, will be joining y'all in the meetin'. You sure are lucky to be working with him. He is such a hunk." She looked at Katie with dreamy eyes.

Katie sat uncomfortably, not sure how to respond to such a comment. She knew her interpersonal skills weren't that great, but then again, you didn't really need interpersonal skills to solve crimes. You just needed intelligence and drive and the ability to interpret body language and evidence. Besides, this woman was very pregnant. Why was she checking out other men? Then again, Katie didn't know that Michael was another man, perhaps he was the father of Jessie's baby. Katie was saved from the uncomfortable situation by the arrival of the man she had passed in the stairwell and another man she had never seen before.

"Um, good luck with, um, everything?" Katie stumbled out to Jessie as she stood to greet the two men.

"We didn't get a chance to introduce ourselves before; I'm Michael Powell," the man from the stairwell said as he stretched out his hand. Michael stood a little over six feet tall with broad shoulders and a narrow waist. His jet-black hair was a longer version of the typical men's style, and curled slightly around his ears. His eyes were a deep chocolate brown, so dark that you couldn't distinguish the pupil from the iris, again reminding her of melted chocolate. He gave Katie a smile that normally made women swoon.

Still confused by the uncomfortable exchange with Jessie, it took Katie a few seconds longer than normal to reach out and shake Michael's hand. As she reached out, her purse fell from her arm to the floor. She bent down to retrieve it at the same time as Michael causing her head to slam into his. "Sorry," she mumbled as she grabbed the strap of her purse and stood back up.

"And I'm Nick Perry," the second man said, extending his hand. Nick's hair was in a military buzz cut. It appeared to be blonde and his eyes were a dull green. Nick stood stiff, probably due to years of military training. His every movement seemed calculated and precise. He was the exact opposite of Michael in every way. Even his black suit with a starched white shirt pointed out the differences between the two men.

Red with embarrassment, Katie reached out and shook his hand a bit overzealously. Nick pulled his hand back and waved her into the office before him and Michael. As she passed Jessie, Katie couldn't help but notice the other woman's compressed lips. It took a second for her to register that Jessie's expression wasn't from labor pains, but from her effort to not laugh at Katie. As Katie walked by, Jessie picked up a stack of papers from her desk and fanned herself, giving Katie an "I told you so" look with a sly glance back at Michael.

Giving herself a mental shake, Katie stepped into the office and approached the man at the desk. The sunlight shining in from the window lit his silver hair, making it look like a halo. The expression on his face said he was anything other than an angel.

"I'm Katie Freeman," she said in a clear voice as she extended her hand.

"Nice to meet you. Marty Nelson. Have a seat." SAC Nelson waved to a round table surrounded by four chairs in the corner, then got up to join the three of them, every move as brisk as his tone. Once everyone was seated, Nelson began by opening Katie's personnel file. "So you are joining our Field Investigation Unit here at the Criminal Investigative Division. What brings you here from Louisiana?"

Katie hadn't been sure what to expect from this first meeting, but an interview question had not even entered her thoughts. She already had the job. She had been told of the transfer by her former SAC in Baton Rouge and packed up her life to move to Tennessee. "Well, I was told I was being transferred. I guess I just thought that was how the Bureau worked. So here I am." Katie had never been good at interviews, mostly because she didn't like being the center of attention. She could easily study other people and identify their emotions and motives, but she could never really be comfortable enough around others to relax and just talk. She was much happier when the conversation was about work, not about her.

The frown on the three faces looking back at her was her first indication that something was wrong. "So, you think the Bureau transferred you here?" Nick Perry asked.

"Well, yes. I had a nearly 100% closure rate at my last station, so I know my work was up to standards. I guess I just thought the Bureau could use my skills elsewhere." Katie tried her best not to squirm or break eye contact.

"How about your partner," Nelson glanced down at the file, though Katie had a feeling he already knew the information he was looking for, "Grady King?"

"What about him?"

"Did the two of you get along?"

"Well, we worked well together. We had great statistics. Is there something specific you want to know?"

"Agent Freeman, what I want to know is why your former SAC requested the Bureau transfer you when, up to this point, your work exceeds the standards of other agents in the division?" Nelson's tone was stern, his gray eyebrows wiggling up and down.

Katie was taken aback by the information. She hadn't known that the transfer was the result of her SAC's request. She sat there for a few minutes with her mouth dropped open as she absorbed the information. "I really don't know why he requested the transfer. I think if you want the answer to that question, you will have to ask him."

"Oh, I did. All he said was that you had done as much as you could in that district and that you needed the experience in other areas to, and I quote, fully round out your personnel file, end of quote. Seems he had nothing negative to say, but also nothing positive.

That to me screams of a problem, Agent. What do you have to say about that?"

Looking Nelson straight in the eye, her own green eyes flashed fire. Katie worked hard to control her temper as she replied, "I have nothing to say to that. If he felt I had achieved all I was able to achieve in their small district, then I am happy to try a new area. Experience is experience, regardless of where it comes from. I am a hard working agent and will do as good a job here, if not better." Sitting back in her chair, Katie continued to look each man in the eye.

Finally, after a few tense moments, ASAC Perry said, "Michael will show you around the building and get you set up in your space. I'm sure you'll hit the ground running."

With that, all three men stood up from the table. Katie quickly followed suit and trailed Michael from the room. Neither of them said a word as they walked down the hall and turned into an office with two desks crammed into it. The desks were butted against each other with the computer monitors facing out, so that each occupant would be looking at the other when seated. The walls were painted institutional beige, but at least there was a small window in the far wall. Michael stepped aside to allow Katie into the office, closing the door behind her. At the sound of the door closing, Katie's heart and breathing sped up. *Get control, Katie. It's not that small of a room.* Despite the internal pep talk, Katie broke out into a sweat. Michael moved around her and took the desk to the right. Quietly, Katie reached back and opened the door a small bit before taking the seat at the other desk. Michael just watched her.

Sitting down, Katie put her purse in the bottom drawer of the desk, checked the other drawers to see what supplies were there and adjusted the height of the chair. Finally, she looked up to see that Michael still hadn't taken his eyes off of her. She simply returned his stare. What was it with the guys in this office staring at her?

"They think you slept with your last partner. That it went bad and you had to be moved," he said.

The sentence was uttered quietly and with no inflection of accusation. It was just a statement.

"I didn't sleep with my last partner, despite his attempts to change that fact. I am here to do my job. I am not here to find a husband and pop out two-point-five kids. I enjoy investigating and I enjoy the challenge of a new case. Are we going to have a problem?" Katie kept her tone even as she responded, though her heart had dropped to her stomach and she felt sick from the implications. Her reputation was important to her, as she had worked so hard to maintain a professional demeanor. To think that one move by a superior could call that into question was nauseating.

"No problems here," Michael replied. "Though I don't think I said anything about a husband or kids." His half-smile was an indication that he was joking. Katie reluctantly smiled back.

CHAPTER TWO

Michael stood up and headed for the office door. "Let's introduce you to the rest of the team and show you the lay of the land." He glanced back to see if Katie was following and proceeded to walk out the door.

Katie quickly caught up as he turned left and headed down the hall.

"It's time for the two o'clock break," Michael continued. Seeing her confusion, Michael explained: "At two every afternoon, anyone in the building gathers in the break room to go over anything interesting that has happened. We toss around ideas from different cases, help each other out when someone is stumped about where to turn next. Basically, just an informal meeting and shoot-the-shit gathering. If nothing business related is happening, we talk sports or stuff. It's a great way for you to meet everyone."

Katie wasn't reassured by his easy smile. She bit back the panic at having to walk into a room full of strangers and be the focus of attention. She was much more of a behind-the-scenes person. Luckily when she stepped into the room there were only two other people there.

"Katie, meet Lucy Boggs and Andy Dillon. They work mostly with cyber crimes. Andy, Lucy, meet Katie."

Lucy was at least six feet tall and very large boned. Her red hair was cropped close to her scalp and when she extended her hand her voice was as deep as Michael's. "Nice to meet you, you new, where'd you come from?" This was all said in one breath and strung together so quickly that Katie had difficulty processing it. The nearly bone-crushing handshake didn't help matters, either.

"I just got here today. I came from the Baton Rouge office in Louisiana," Katie replied, with what she hoped was a small enough pause to not be noticeable.

Lucy's booming laughter filled up the entire break room. "Guess I will have to slow my speech for ya. Them folks down there talk r-e-e-e-al slow," Lucy replied with another booming laugh.

"Don't let Lucy run you off. I'm Andy." As Katie shook his hand she took in his small stature. Standing a few inches shorter than she, Andy had blonde hair and hazel eyes. He could have passed for an eighteen-year-old, but there was a sadness in his eyes that aged him. His presence immediately put Katie at ease.

Truly smiling for the first time that day, Katie shook his hand and asked what exactly he did for cyber crimes.

"Oh, Lucy and I look for child pornography and online predators. In fact, it's about to be our busy time of day. We look forward to the two o'clock break just to get us pumped up for what will be a very disturbing few hours." Seeing the confusion on Katie's face, he continued, "School lets out at 2:30 around here. But, as you know, the standard workday doesn't end until 5:00. That two-and-a-half hour block is when children are left alone with their computers and the Internet, just waiting for mom or dad to get home.

Predators know this and they use it. Lucy and I get the pleasure of going online and posing as twelve-year-olds to see what sickos are out there looking for us. " The last bit was said with obvious distaste, but it went a long way toward explaining the look behind his eyes.

Lucy spoke up in a sobered voice, "The rest of the day is better. At least we get a break from the slime when we get pulled into one of your cases. It always makes for a better day to catch someone preying on adults." Michael and Andy snorted out laughs, breaking the heaviness in the room.

The four of them continued talking for a few moments before Andy and Lucy left to become child victims of online predators. Over the next thirty minutes, several other agents came in and introduced themselves. Michael must have sensed Katie's insecurity because he never left her to fend for herself. She learned a lot about how the office interrelated and also learned that Michael was not the father of Jessie's baby. There was an office betting pool going for the delivery date and weight of the baby. Katie didn't join, she had no idea how to predict delivery dates and even less of an idea about a newborn's weight.

Finally at three, they made their way down the corridor with Michael pointing out the copy room, the supply room and the bathrooms before finally returning to their office. This time, he didn't completely close the door. Katie smiled internally when she noticed the gesture.

Returning to their seats, Michael slid four folders across his desk and onto hers. "These are four unsolved cold cases. My old partner, Stan, retired last month. These are four of his cases from before I came that he left for me to hopefully complete. Of course, those are the condensed versions. The full files are in the basement storage room, which we will spare you the introduction to as long as humanly possible."

Katie was getting used to his easy smile and manner. It would take her a while to loosen up, but at least he wasn't holding Nelson and Perry's assumptions over her head.

"So, where are you from?" Michael asked.

"Why do you want to know?" The short reply was out of her mouth before Katie could stop it.

"Well, um, I just thought we could get to know each other a bit, seeing as we'll be working so closely together. Your accent isn't from Louisiana, so I am assuming that you didn't grow up there," Michael said uncertainly. The frown was back on his face, and he obviously didn't know what he had said wrong.

Katie sighed. "You're right. I didn't grow up there. I didn't mean to be so short with you."

"Short comes naturally to the vertically challenged," Michael said, his easy smile returning and causing Katie to roll her eyes. "But you didn't answer my question. Where is your family?"

"I don't have family," Katie said vaguely.

"Ok, how can a person not have family?"

"I never knew my dad and my mom and I parted ways when I left home at eighteen," Katie said, her tone meant to close the subject.

"Guess you don't like to talk about you." Michael said. "Tell you what, I'm gonna tell you all about me. And maybe each morning, you can tell me one fact about yourself. Then maybe we can get to know each other. I just think it makes our working relationship better if we know how the other operates. I'm an open book. Feel free to ask me anything."

Despite her better judgment, Katie was really curious about her new partner. So she decided to play along. "Where did you come from? Where is your family?" Starting by throwing his two questions back at him, Katie smirked and waited to see what he would say.

"Now, see, is that so hard? Well, I am from the great city of Smyrna. That's just south of here. I still live there. So do my mom and dad and all seven of my siblings."

"You have *seven* siblings?" Katie's response was a combination of shock and longing.

"Yup. Three brothers and four sisters. My parents joke that they should have tried for one more each, then they could have had two starting line-ups. We are all tall and athletic. We all played basketball in high school and a few of us in college too."

"Where did you go to college? Were you one of the ones who played in college? What do your siblings do?" Despite herself, Katie couldn't stop the flow of questions. She was an only child and had lived such a sheltered and secluded life. This family was a foreign concept to her.

Michael laughed at her enthusiasm. "Yes, I played college basketball for the University of Tennessee. I got my degree in Sociology, with an emphasis on Criminal Justice. I then went to Law School at UT and then joined the FBI."

Michael stopped talking and though he didn't ask any follow ups, it was obvious that he was curious as to what sparked the questions.

"You didn't answer about what your siblings do."

"Well, most of them work in the family landscaping business. Two of my sisters are stay-at-home moms." Michael laughed at Katie's scrunched up nose. She had no desire to be a stay-at-home anything, as evidenced by her earlier comment about kids.

"Why didn't you join the family business?"

"Well, I went to college with the intention of studying landscape design or some such thing. But criminal justice caught my attention when I took a freshman sociology course. I just knew from that moment on that I wanted to be in law enforcement."

Again, he didn't ask anything more from her, but this time, she felt obligated to share something in return "I'm an only child. I was raised by my mom in Arizona. It wouldn't have been so lonely to have had other family."

"Woo hoo! Now that wasn't so tough, was it?" Michael's outburst made Katie jump and then laugh as she realized that he had lured her into the conversation with the express purpose of breaking her exterior.

"I'm not very good at sharing," Katie admitted.

"Well, that didn't really need to be said." Michael winked at her to soften the comment. "I'll help you work on that." With that, he stood up again and headed for the door. "What do you say we call it a day and reconvene tomorrow at 0800?"

"That sounds nice. So can I ask you one more question?" At his affirmative nod, she asked, "Could you recommend a good place to stay? I just got into town about thirty minutes before our meeting, so I don't know the lay of the land yet."

"You don't have a place to stay?" he asked incredulously.

"Nope, just me and my suitcases in the car. I figured I would find a place once I learned the city a bit and knew which area to live in. Until then, I thought I could stay in a hotel. Free breakfast, right?" Her smile was nervous, but at least she was attempting to interact.

"I know just the place. Why don't you let me drive you and pick you up in the morning?" Michael new immediately that was the wrong thing to say. Katie's face closed so quick it was like a slamming door.

"Never mind, I'll find a hotel nearby."

Michael sighed, "I'm sorry," he said. "I didn't mean to make you uncomfortable. Why don't you follow me? Traffic can be a little hairy, so I was just trying to spare you the headache in an unfamiliar city. I know a great bed-and-breakfast in Smyrna. It will put you further from the craziness, and since I already live down there and the administration tries to give me cases down that direction, I figure it would be good for you to be south as well."

Katie nodded, relieved that he seemed to understand without her having to explain. They got into their cars and headed south.

CHAPTER THREE

Michael led Katie to a yellow Victorian house nestled on about twenty acres on the outskirts of Smyrna. Smyrna was a city of a little over 40,000 people located about half an hour south of Nashville in Rutherford County. Katie immediately felt at home. Though the house she grew up in had been pueblo style, it too was situated on a lot of land on the outskirts of town. For the first time in a long time, Katie experienced a pang of homesickness.

Inside, Katie met Caroline Shoulders, the owner of the bed and breakfast and her three children, Ian, Tommy and Carrie. She signed in and went to settle into her new room. The room was decorated in shades of maroon and cream. The furniture was dark mahogany and oversized. Looking out the window, Katie had a beautiful view of the lake on the back of the property. Sighing, she sat down at the window seat and allowed her mind to drift back to her childhood home. She didn't like to think about it much; it always made her sad. Though the bed-and-breakfast felt like home, the scenery was very different. The trees outside the window were green with lush green pastures in the outlying fields. Back home, there wasn't much grass and the few trees they had were different from the dense foliage here. Finally, she shook herself back to the present and got up to unpack her belongings.

Katie came down for dinner at the appointed time and met Caroline's husband, Kevin. Kevin worked as an accountant for a local firm and coached little league for both his boys. Carrie was only three, and didn't yet play. Dinner was a boisterous event, with all the kids trying to tell about their day. The Shoulders offered to serve Katie in the private dining room intended for guests, but as she was currently the only one staying at the B&B, Katie chose to sit with the family. Secretly she was interested to see how families interacted. Katie offered to help clean up the dishes, but Caroline wouldn't hear of having a guest work in the kitchen, so instead she changed into her running clothes and decided to take a run around the property.

Retiring to her room, Katie showered, then pulled out her notebook and wrote a letter to her mother. She didn't know if her mother even read them, or if she just threw them in the trash when they came in the mail. Regardless, it made her feel better - or at least connected to something in the world - to write home. She always mailed them and always would, as long as they didn't come back unopened. More than likely, it was Patty, the woman who helped run the ranch, who read them, rather than her mom, but that was okay. She owed Patty more than she could ever repay. While she wrote the letters, she always pictured her mother sitting on the veranda sipping iced tea and having lemon cookies while reading them. It never failed to make her cry, though she would never let anyone see her tears. *Tears are a sign of weakness. You must keep your emotions inside. If you show them to people, they will take advantage.* Her mother's words came back to her as if the woman were sitting right beside her saying them.

Finishing her letter, Katie called it a night and crawled into bed. The minute the lights were out, she fell into a deep dreamless sleep. Her mind recognized the place as home and, for once, didn't keep her up tormenting her with all her mistakes.

Michael arrived at the B&B at 7:30 the next morning. He was sitting at the dining room table eating breakfast when Katie came downstairs.

"What are you doing here?" she asked abruptly. Then seeming to catch her tone, especially in front of Caroline, she added, "I didn't expect to see you until I got to the office. I think I can find my way now."

"I have no doubt you can find your way, but we have a case down south, so I thought I would stop by and we could take off from here," he replied. "Have some breakfast and then we'll head out."

Normally eager to start her day, Katie was about to turn down the offer, but her stomach chose that moment to be heard. Caroline turned from the stove with a plate piled with eggs, bacon, a biscuit and jelly, and some white substance. "What's that?" Katie asked, pointing to the semi-liquid stuff.

"Don't tell me you've never eaten grits?" Michael chortled. His amusement with her was growing by the day.

"I've never seen grits, but I have heard of them. Are they good?"

"Give them a try," Caroline said. "And don't mind him, he just likes to aggravate people. Comes from being the almost youngest."

"Oh, did you two grow up together?"

At the odd look that Caroline gave Michael, Katie knew she had missed some connection. Just then six-year-old Tommy rushed into the room. "Guess what, Uncle Michael? I lost my first tooth!" he crowed as he threw himself onto Michael's lap. Katie's fork paused halfway to her mouth. Slowly lowering the fork back to the plate, she looked up at Caroline.

"Thank you for the hospitality. I will look for another place to stay this evening." Katie shook her head. She should have seen the family resemblance. All the kids and Caroline had the same dark hair and brown eyes as Michael. Now that she looked, Ian could have passed for Michael's son instead of his nephew.

"Please don't do that. My brother is always trying to play Mr. Fix-It. The truth is, we just opened as a B&B and you are our second guest. He's trying to help us get our name out, and having a long-term guest is great for business. I'm sorry he didn't tell you. If I had known, I would have told you myself last night. Besides, with you here, we can share Michael stories." The look on Caroline's face showed how much the family needed the business, and since the place felt like home, Katie reluctantly nodded and resumed eating. Caroline glared at her brother and turned to the stove to dish out food for the kids as they came down. Each one jumped on Michael's lap and told him all the newest information. It was such a homey scene that Katie had to swallow several times to get rid of the lump in her throat.

Half an hour later, Michael and Katie left the B&B to head to Shelbyville, a small town about forty-five minutes south, where Elaine Henderson, a wife and mother of two, had been abducted the week before. Earlier that morning, the husband had gone out to retrieve the morning paper and found his wife's nude and mutilated body on the front porch. When the local police saw what had been done, they immediately called for FBI assistance.

Shelbyville was the county seat for Bedford County and was known for Tennessee Walking Horses and making pencils. About half the county population lived within the city of Shelbyville, or about 16,000 people. Sitting on the banks of the Duck River, it was a sleepy little town that prided itself on being family friendly. The only excitement in town was usually when the Tennessee Walking Horse National Celebration was held.

There was one police car blocking off each end of the street where the Hendersons lived. The home was a two-story Cape Cod with little doghouse-shaped windows protruding from the roof and a porch that stretched end-to-end. It sat at the end of a long drive on a hill that overlooked the neighborhood. Michael and Katie flashed their identification and were allowed through. Michael pulled the car up to the curb noting that there were two police cars in the driveway, unconsciously destroying possible evidence. Exchanging a knowing look with Katie, they emerged from the car and went up to the front porch.

As they approached, they noticed there was a lump on the porch that had been covered with a blanket. "Chief Davidson at your service," a portly man said, as he approached them from one of the cars; his large cowboy hat obscured most of his face. They introduced themselves, shook hands and asked for a briefing.

"Well, now, I reckon that seeing it would be easier to believe than trying to describe it. Truth is, I just don't know as I got words to put to this." The older man was scratching his bald head as he shook it. He was highly distressed and the jerky movements showed how upsetting the situation was for him. "I been in law enforcement for nigh on forty years and ain't never seen nuthin' ta equal it. I had my men put the blanket over her. Just don't seem right leaving that out for all the eyes that might be lookin'." He replaced his hat on his head and gestured for the agents to go onto the porch, but made no move to follow.

Michael gently lifted the blanket back to reveal a woman with long blonde hair. That was the only identifiable feature, as the rest of her was folded up. Her legs were folded under her and her head was resting between her knees. There was a metal band wrapped around her body, squeezing her tightly. Putting on gloves, Katie gently pushed the hair back from the woman's face. The tear streaks down her face were red, as if she had been crying blood. Without touching anything more, Michael gently replaced the blanket and they went back down the steps to rejoin the chief.

"Who coulda done that to poor Elaine? She never hurt nobody," the chief said.

"You knew the victim?" Katie asked.

"Her name is Elaine, not the victim. She's my wife." The anguished statement came from the backseat of the nearest patrol car. It was the only thing the man could say as he broke down sobbing. He buried is face in his hands, his bathrobe gaping open across his chest.

"I am sorry for your loss, Mr. Henderson. I promise we will do everything we can to find the person responsible," Michael said. He motioned for the chief to follow him out of hearing range of Mr. Henderson. "We need the background on this case. Everything from the time she was abducted. I don't know what that device is but we will find out."

"It's called The Scavenger's Daughter," Katie said. "It's a medieval torture device that was around in the sixteenth century." Both men just turned and stared. "I have a degree in history. I combined it with my criminal justice degree and did a thesis on medieval crime and punishment. I know a lot about this subject; let's suffice to say that the death wasn't pretty."

"Did she suffer long?" the chief asked.

"Well, it's too soon to tell right now. The device can be quick or it can be prolonged over a period of days. Judging from her condition, I would say she has been dead for no more than six hours, but the coroner will have to confirm that. I also know that if she was abducted a week ago, and has only been deceased for six hours, she had to suffer some." Hopefully not like this for that entire time, Katie added to herself.

The chief just shook his head. "How am I supposed to tell Rick that? That's his wife up there."

"Actually, we would appreciate it if you didn't tell him how she died." Michael said. "We would like to keep that fact quiet as long as possible. How many people have seen the body?"

"Well, Rick saw it, the two deputies who answered the 911 call, and myself. You two and whoever the coroner sends. That would be it."

"Let's try to keep it that way. It might be wise to ask your men to keep this confidential. That means not even telling their spouse," Katie said in a flat tone. Though she didn't intend to be brisk, her manner came across that way. She hadn't grown up learning to sugarcoat her words and saw no reason to now.

The chief puffed out his chest prepared to jump to the defense of his men. Michael quickly stepped in and said, "We all know that they are aware of the need to keep this confidential, but something this upsetting, especially to someone they know, can lead to a need to talk. Please just remind them that if they need to talk, they should do so to a licensed professional and not at home." The chief deflated at Michael's words and walked off to talk to his deputies.

Michael turned back to Katie. "Luckily, the Bedford County medical examiner is very competent. She should be here any minute now." As he finished speaking, the medical examiner's van pulled up and Dr. Marie Bennett stepped out. The tiny woman with spiky salt-and-pepper hair approached Michael and shook his hand.

"Heard old Stan retired. About damn time." Turning to Katie, she extended her hand, "I'm Marie, sorry to meet you under these circumstances." Energy vibrated from her small frame and she seemed to be perpetually in motion.

Katie extended her hand introducing herself at the same time. "How much do you know about medieval torture?" Katie asked.

Looking surprised, Marie answered, "Not a thing. Is that a trick question?"

"Unfortunately not," Katie replied. "The victim was left on the front porch in a device called The Scavenger's Daughter. What I didn't tell the chief is that the device isn't necessarily used to bring about death. Normally the victim is squeezed until their ribs and breastbone break. Sometimes the spine dislocates. It can cause great damage, even the bleeding in the eyes due to the pressure exerted on the internal organs. The victims usually die slowly from internal injuries. My educated guess is that she was left on the porch still alive. I think it was a game to the guy, maybe a 'let's see if the husband finds her in time.'"

Michael and Marie just stared back at Katie in horror. Finally, Marie managed to say something. "That is horrible. Are you serious? Who would do that?" Marie looked up to the covered lump on the porch, shaking her head.

"A very sick and twisted individual," Michael answered as he too looked at the covered lump on the porch. Without another word, the three of them turned and climbed the steps to begin the process of removing the body.

CHAPTER FOUR

The three of them spent the next several hours photographing the scene and collecting evidence. After having the police vehicles removed from the driveway, much to the embarrassment of Chief Davidson, Michael and Katie worked to identify any signs of the person who had left Mrs. Henderson on her own porch. The only visible signs of a vehicle were from a tire imprint by the sidewalk.

"It appears he backed his vehicle up to the steps to remove Mrs. Henderson. Let's get a cast of the imprint. Might help us out later," Michael speculated, rubbing the back of his neck. They had been stooped down duck-walking over every inch of the driveway and front yard for over three hours at this point and the temperature had climbed to the low eighties. "Let's let the crime scene people finish up here. I want to get down to the morgue and check out the autopsy." Michael's comment showed his distaste for the process. The medical examiner's van had pulled out over an hour before, taking Mrs. Henderson to her final injustice.

"I think autopsies are fascinating," Katie said. "They always reveal so much about a person. It's like all your secrets are just there to be discovered. The closet smoker who never wanted the family to know…you can't hide the evidence provided by your lungs. The woman who had a secret child…she can no longer hide the evidence of giving birth." There was a reverence in Katie's tone as she spoke. "Of course, there are the disturbing ones, like Mrs. Henderson, who will have the secrets of what was done to her exposed. I'm sure she would be embarrassed by it all, but in the end, it will be those secrets that will allow us to find who did this to her. Guess it doesn't really mean much to her at this point..." Her voice trailed off at the end, as she gazed out over the street. Television and camera crews had begun to show up over the course of the morning. They were scrambling to get any information they could. Luckily the body had been removed in time to prevent any long-range lenses that might have captured the indignity.

The two went into the house through the back door to talk to Chief Davidson and let him know they would be in touch after they had sifted through the existing case file and gotten the results of the autopsy and the findings from the scene. Rick Henderson was sitting with the chief at the eat-in kitchen table staring into a cup of coffee that had long gone cold. He had managed to switch out his bathrobe for a t-shirt, but still had on the pajama pants and house slippers he was wearing earlier.

Finishing his discussion with the chief, Michael sat down beside Rick. "I'm very sorry for your loss. Are you up to answering a few questions for us?" His tone was gentle, but it was clear that it wasn't really a question. Rick just nodded his head without looking up; his slumped shoulders projecting his exhaustion and pain. He was a man destroyed by the events of the past week.

"Can you walk us through the last day that your wife was here?"

Sighing, it seemed to take all the remaining energy for Rick to begin talking. "It was Wednesday. Wednesday is always her personal day. See, with her staying at home with the kids all the time, she needs a few hours to recharge. On Wednesday, she leaves here when I get home about five, goes to church, gives her confession, works with the ladies on whatever project is coming up. She's usually home around ten. Last Wednesday, they would've been working on the upcoming beginning-of-summer yard sale. All the families in the parish went through their closets to see what they could donate. The proceeds go toward helping kids that can't afford to go to summer church camp. Elaine is a natural leader, so she's generally one of the people in charge. She is always one of the last to leave, but the parking lot behind the church is well lit so we don't worry about it too much. Besides, they always left in groups. That night, Elaine walked out with her sister Evelyn. They're twins. Oh Lord, this is gonna destroy Evelyn. Has anyone told her?" Rick lifted his tear-stained face to Chief Davidson, looking for an answer to his question.

Chief Davidson nodded. "We sent Bobby over as soon as we knew it was her. Evelyn is keeping the kids away from the television for a few days. She said she would wait to tell them until you were there."

At this news, Rick broke down sobbing again. "How am I supposed to tell my kids that their mom died? I couldn't even tell them she was missing. I just told them she went on a trip for a little while and sent them to stay with Evelyn. Evie said she needed them close, that it made Elaine seem not so far away. How am I supposed to do this?"

The three of them sat there in silence while Rick calmed down and collected himself. Finally, he was able to continue. "Evelyn said Elaine couldn't find her keys in her purse. She was just gonna run back into the church and see if she left them inside. While she waited, Father Joe came out and talked to her for a few minutes. It was taking so long that Evelyn and Father Joe went back in to see what was going on. The table with the kids' toys was turned over, but Elaine wasn't anywhere to be found. Father Joe called the police."

Chief Davidson picked up the story from there. "We talked to all the women who were there that night. Father Joe was questioned, but he didn't see her after he took her confession earlier in the evening. It's like she just vanished into thin air. We searched that church high and low. She just wasn't there."

Michael asked a few more questions as Katie stayed in the background watching body language and listening to the conversation. Figuring they had learned all they could for the time being, Katie and Michael got up and headed for the FBI lab in Nashville to attend the autopsy.

Once in the car, Michael asked, "So what do you think?"

"I think he loved his wife very much." Katie said. "I don't think he had anything to do with what happened. And I'm very interested to see this church and to see how one person can just vanish from inside." Katie pulled out the file and began reading the statements.

"Here's something interesting. Elaine's purse was found on a table just inside the door, but her keys were never found. I wonder what happened to her car?" Katie mused. "The statements from the other women are pretty brief, but then I would expect them to be since they left before Elaine. No one saw anything. Elaine acted normal all evening. No evidence she had just run off. Well, I guess now we know that wasn't the case. Evelyn's is the longest statement in the group, but still doesn't offer insight. I am interested in talking to the priest. He was alone in the church for a few minutes with Elaine. Could he have stashed her somewhere?"

"I don't see how he could," Michael said. "If the entire church was searched within minutes, where could he have put her in the meantime?"

"Good question. I would like to clarify with Evelyn whether or not the good Father was out of her sight between the time they reentered the building and the time the police showed up to search it."

CHAPTER FIVE

Katie looked up as Michael turned into the parking lot of the forensic facility in Nashville. They walked in and were issued visitors passes, which allowed them access to the morgue. The morgue was located on the second level of the facility, the cheery light coming through the windows giving a false sense of peace to a place where death pervaded. The agents entered separate dressing rooms and changed into protective sterile clothing before emerging through the back entrance, which led to the windowless autopsy room.

Mrs. Henderson had already been placed on the stainless steel table. Dr. Bennett and her assistant, Fred, were standing on the other side of the table wearing puzzled expressions under their protective face shields.

"What did you find?" Michael asked from Katie's left. She hadn't heard him emerge from his dressing room. Katie quickly turned back to the body on the table, refusing to acknowledge to herself that Michael looked even better in the blue scrubs he had changed into.

"Well, nothing yet," Dr. Bennett said. "We can't really figure out how to get her out of this contraption. We need to unfold her and get x-rays before we proceed, but in this position, x-rays are nearly impossible."

Katie walked over to the table. "May I?" she asked, gesturing to the sterile gloves behind Fred. He turned and grabbed a pair, handing them across the table to Katie. Pulling them on, Katie reached up and began twisting what looked to be a flower protruding from the top of the band. As she turned it, the others saw that it was a screw and they watched as the band loosened. Once the screw had come out and allowed the band to separate, Dr. Bennett reached out to pull it apart.

"You might want to wait a second," Katie said. "I need to free her hands and feet first." Ignoring the astounded looks being directed at her, Katie located the mechanisms that would allow Elaine's hands to be freed. From there, Katie asked for assistance to unfold the top half of the body back and to bring the knees up so that she could access Elaine's ankles. Finally, forty-five minutes after starting, Elaine lay prone on the table. They all stood looking down at her body and seeing the evidence of additional torture that had been invisible from the crunched position in which she had been found.

Elaine's abdomen and thighs were criss-crossed with welts, some of which had broken the skin. There was bruising around all of them, some yellowed with time and others recently purple and black. There was no blood on the body, aside from that on her face, which had resulted from being squeezed by the device. The blood in her body had pooled in her shins and abdomen as it had settled after her heart stopped pumping.

Fred pulled out the camera and began documenting the findings. Dr. Bennett began her examination at Elaine's feet and worked her way up, taking the necessary samples as she went. She measured the length and depth of the cuts to her extremities and to her abdomen. Looking under her nails, she noted, "There are no defensive wounds and nothing noticeable under the nails. I'll take scrapings just in case, but I don't expect to find anything. There are ligature marks on the wrists that match those on the ankles."

Moving up to her head, Dr. Bennett noted dry, cracked lips. She opened Elaine's mouth and gasped. Moving closer, Katie and Michael looked to see what had caused such a reaction. All of Elaine's teeth were cracked and chipped. Her tongue was swollen and her front two teeth, both upper and lower were broken off. "Looks as though she bit down repeatedly on something hard," Dr. Bennett said.

"Judging from the device we found her in, I would imagine it was probably something similar to The Scold's Bridle." Seeing the blank looks the other three were aiming at her, Katie explained, "It was a device used around the same time as The Scavenger's Daughter. It was used as punishment for wives who nagged their husbands or women who gossiped. It was an iron mask that fitted around the face and generally included some sort of iron gag that was inserted into the mouth. Sometimes the gags were spiked, causing the tongue to bleed continuously. If you think about it, you move your tongue constantly: when you swallow, when you speak, when you eat or drink, or even if you are just sitting around. Your tongue almost never remains still. Now imagine a spike that anchored it to the bottom of your mouth. If you swallow, the spike tears the muscle a bit and it bleeds. If you take a drink, again, it bleeds. What I don't understand is why this guy used *two* instruments that were not specifically designed to kill. He obviously wanted to inflict as much pain as possible. But what message is he sending by using these specific devices? There's no connection between the two. I mean, historically. Usually a nag or gossip was given a sentence, or her husband determined the length of time, that the device was worn. It wasn't generally used in combination with other torture devices. This guy has to be saying something more."

Michael and Katie stepped back to allow Fred and Dr. Bennett to turn Elaine over. Free of the device, it was now clear to see that her back and the backs of her thighs had suffered the same treatment as the front. Once again, Dr. Bennett began her examination at the feet and moved up. Fred took pictures of everything and noted it on the forms. Overhead, the video camera continued to record everything said and done for the official record.

With the external examination completed, Fred pulled the arm of the x-ray machine over the body. Michael, Katie and Dr. Bennett stepped behind the protective wall as Fred went about taking the x-rays. Once he competed the ones of the back, Dr. Bennett assisted him in turning Elaine back over. She once again joined Michael and Katie while Fred resumed his process. The three of them joined Fred on the right side of the room as the images began coming up on the three screens mounted to the wall. They reviewed the x-rays, beginning with views of the skull and moving down the body. There were no broken bones.

Moving to the x-rays of the pelvis, they all noted something inserted in the vaginal cavity. At Katie's sigh, everyone turned to look at her.

"It's called the Pear of Anguish," she said. "It's basically an iron or metal pear shaped device. Once inserted, it is cranked open. It was used as punishment for various crimes. It could be used orally as a punishment for heresy, anally for punishment of homosexuality, or vaginally for adulterers. As it opened, it basically destroyed the muscles around it. Sometimes it also had spikes to maximize the damage caused. I don't see spikes on this x-ray, but I suppose we'll see once it is removed. I can show you how to do that." Katie and Dr. Bennett walked back over to the body. The men stood back, in a show of respect for the victim. Katie bent Elaine's legs and maneuvered them open. Reaching up, she began unscrewing what looked like another flower. As she did this, the device inside slowly closed until eventually she was able to remove it. Neither woman said a word, as Dr. Bennett put the device on a separate tray for Fred to photograph and tag. The women rejoined the men and the somber group completed the view of the x-rays.

Returning to the body, Dr. Bennett was about to begin her internal examination when Michael's phone rang. Excusing himself, he stepped aside to answer the call. After a brief conversation, he ended the call and said, "We have another woman who has been kidnapped in Shelbyville. The Chief asked us to come back down and help out. They're canvassing the area now." After getting Dr. Bennett's assurances that she would forward all her findings to them that afternoon, the two departed.

CHAPTER SIX

Needing to clear her mind from the horror she had just witnessed, Katie pulled out one of the cold case files from her briefcase. "Tell me about the Henry Stephens case," she said to Michael. She flipped through the file as Michael began to talk.

"Well, about twenty-five years ago, Henry Stephens - known to his friends as Hank - was found shot to death in his home. His wife, Charlene was nowhere to be found. The police searched for weeks for her, but it was as if she disappeared into thin air."

"How did this become an FBI case? I don't see why the locals would ask for our assistance for a single unsolved murder."

"That's where the Stephens murder is weird. His tox screen came back positive for alcohol and OxyContin. Hank was known as a hard-core opponent of drug use. He had forbidden his wife from hanging out with some of her family because they were known users or dealers. In fact, her cousin Billy Sheppard was arrested the night of the murder for attempting to sell Oxy to an undercover officer. Oxy was just coming to be known as a problem on the streets, so the locals were really cracking down on anyone caught selling it. Billy was found with over eighty pills on him. The locals turned to our drug unit for help. They wanted to try to stop this in its tracks before there was a full-blown epidemic in their city. Billy refused to say where he got the drugs, so he was tried and convicted. The strange thing is that he was offered a deal; he could either name his source, or he could work as a snitch and let the cops find his source through watching him. He still refused. They all knew that Billy was small-time. It never made sense to anyone that he wouldn't name his supplier. Then Hank's body was found and everyone looked to Billy. Lucky for him, Billy was in jail at the time of the murder. The cops tried every which way to Sunday to get him to talk. Instead, he chose to serve his two years and then went about his business. He's never gotten in trouble again, seems to lead a clean life. We stop by every now and again to see if he's had a change of heart, but to date, he never has."

Katie was silent for a few minutes, processing all that Michael had said. She continued to flip through the pages. "Hang on one second. You said he was shot to death? If he was so opposed to drugs, then it's probably safe to say he didn't voluntarily ingest the Oxy. So why drug him and then shoot him?"

"Hmm, never thought of it that way. We all just assumed his distaste for anything drug-related was a front for him actually taking drugs."

"Isn't there a way to know about long term drug use?" Katie asked.

"That's a good question. Might be something we can look up when we get back to the office. I do know that OxyContin causes euphoria. Hard to imagine a man who's happy beating his wife as often as Hank seemed to beat Charlene. She was in the hospital almost more than she was out."

A slight "hmm" was the only reply. They rode the rest of the way in silence. An hour and a half after leaving the morgue, they turned onto a residential street in Shelbyville. The houses were run down and the yards in disrepair. More than one boasted cars on blocks and at the far end was a trailer in desperate need of attention. It looked like a stiff breeze could blow it down. The yard was securely fenced with several Beware of Dog signs posted along the side. This seemed to be the center of activity. Pulling up to the trailer, Michael and Katie emerged from the car and once again greeted Chief Davidson.

"What makes you think this disappearance is related to the Henderson kidnapping?" Katie asked once they had exchanged greetings.

"Well, for one thing, Barbie Jones volunteers with Elaine at Christ the King. For another, she disappeared from the park that backs up to church property. We've been out canvassing damn near the whole town. Still no sign of her," Chief Davidson said.

"No offense, but serial kidnappers and murderers generally have a certain type. They look the same or have a similar socioeconomic status, something to tie them together." Katie's tone was sharp.

It had only taken Michael half a day to realize that social interaction and sensitivity weren't Katie's forte. He gently stepped in to take over questioning, silently hoping that the two of them could form a relationship that worked. He already knew he admired her mind. She saw things differently. Perhaps keeping her on the evidence and him on the interviews would help the investigation. "What else can you tell us about Ms. Jones that might connect her disappearance to Elaine's?" he asked. Michael instinctually knew that he would get more from the chief if he kept the women's names front and center.

"Well, Barbie - full name Barbara Ann Jones - was born and raised here. Hell, my son went to high school with her. Even dated her for a while right after. She always had eyes for Chuck, though. That girl was plumb crazy about him."

"I believe Elaine was thirty-eight, correct? How old is Barbie?" Michael asked.

"I would put her about thirty or so. Let's see... DeWayne, my son, just turned thirty-one, so that would be about right."

Nodding, Michael motioned toward the trailer. "Think we can go in and talk to the husband?" At the chief's nod, the three of them headed inside. The minute they walked through the door, three pit bulls stood to their feet and stared at them. The dogs didn't growl or bark, but their stance was obviously protective of their master.

"Sit," came the quiet command from the man sitting at the kitchen table. "Are you the feds? You gonna find my wife?" Despite the look of the outside of the trailer, the inside was immaculate. It was obvious that someone had taken good care of the furnishings inside, even though they were in threadbare conditions. There wasn't a speck of dust or dirt to be found. Even with three dogs in the house, there was no pet hair anywhere. On the end tables, the lamps sat on crocheted doilies. The headrest of the recliner sported an enlarged version of the doily.

"What can you tell us about your wife's routine today, Mr. Jones?" Michael gently asked as he sat next to the man. Katie continued to wander around the house.

"Well, she fixed me breakfast before work. I knew she had to drop off some stuff at the church. She usually went to the park when she was over to that side of town. See, she wanted kids, but the good Lord ain't seen fit to give us none. She always went over to watch the kids play. Said the laughter encouraged her soul. Please find her before he does something bad to her." His pleading tone was heartbreaking.

Michael worked hard to keep his expression neutral. He had just seen first-hand what this man did to his victims. There was no way he was going to reveal that information to another victim's husband.

Katie had been looking at all the pictures on the wall. There was one of a happy couple on their wedding day surrounded by a lot of family. The wall itself was covered in framed photographs that progressed in age from left to right. The last photo on the right was of a couple with a dead deer between them. The man was Chuck Jones. "Is this Barbie?" Katie asked. Chuck looked up and nodded when he saw the picture she was pointing to. Barbie was a tiny blonde haired woman. Standing next to her husband, she looked even smaller. Katie would put her at approximately five feet two inches and barely a hundred pounds.

Chuck appeared by her side. "We took that picture over the winter. It was her first deer. She'd been bugging me to teach her to shoot since we got married. But she's so small and fragile that I didn't want her to learn. Made me feel good knowing I could provide for her. See, we don't have much, but we love each other. That was always enough for her. Don't know why she chose me. There were lots o' men who could give her better. She has to be okay." The last statement was made in an anguished whisper.

Picking up on something he said, Katie asked, "What do you mean she's fragile?" The woman in the picture might be small, but there was an attitude about her that screamed anything but fragile.

Chuck grunted a small laugh. "Don't tell her I said that. She would whip my butt into next week." Seeming to realize what he said, Chuck shook his head and continued. "She has diabetes, type one. Has had it all her life. Before, doctors always said not to try to have kids. But nowadays, they think it's okay. Her sugar has been under control all her life, 'cept for once in high school. She decided she was tired of bein' different so she stopped taking her insulin. She nearly went into a coma before her ma caught what she was doing." Chuck shook his head at the memory and shuffled back to his seat at the table.

Michael poured him a glass of water while asking, "Any idea when she took her last insulin dose, and when her next one is due?"

"Well, I know she took one this morning. She keeps some supplies in her purse, but she don't like taking it in public, so mostly she stays at home to inject herself. She has to take her sugar levels before eating. Her lunch is still in the fridge, so I don't think she made it home for lunch. She's way past due for a dose by now." The worry on his face was plain.

"We're going to go check in with the searchers. The chief will stay with you, so he can keep you up to date on what's happening." Michael stood and he and Katie left the trailer.

Pulling the chief aside, Katie said, "Make sure someone stays here overnight. We don't want another woman left on the front porch where her husband finds her. It would also be good to have someone here to catch the guy making the drop. I think Mrs. Jones will be brought back sooner than Mrs. Henderson was." The chief just nodded and Michael and Katie turned to leave.

"This isn't good," Michael said the minute they were outside.

"Guess that depends on your perspective," Katie said. "If she passes out or goes into a coma, she won't have to suffer what Elaine Henderson did."

Michael thanked the stars above that Katie hadn't expressed that thought in front of Chuck Jones.

They drove to the park behind Christ the King church, which was serving as the headquarters for the search parties. It seemed that the whole town was there to help out. There were so many vehicles in both the park and the church parking lot that Michael had to park nearly a block away. Walking the rest of the way, Michael and Katie entered the back door of the church. The door opened into a wide hallway with six doors spaced evenly, three on each side. At the far end, opposite the entry, was a seventh door. They made their way to the table at the other side of the first room on the left to check in with the deputies manning the maps and assigning search quadrants.

Once Michael was in conversation with the deputies, Katie walked away to look around the church. In the room across the hall there were several tables in rows, each piled high with various items. On the near side, there were tables of clothing, which appeared to be arranged by size and gender. In the next row, there were tables with household decorations and knick-knacks. The table farthest from the door held children's toys and wasn't arranged as neatly as the rest. Remembering that this table had been overturned during the timeframe before Elaine Henderson had been discovered missing, Katie began to look at it more closely. One of the legs was bent and she made a note to ask if it had been that way before the kidnapping. Moving on, she paced the room trying to picture how the attack had happened.

Imagining she was the kidnapper, she threw a large duffle bag over her shoulder and walked from the toy table to the door, attempting not to bump into any of the other tables. The aisles were narrow and it wasn't possible to make it to the doorway, which was the only exit to the room, without hitting several of the other tables.

She was almost to the door when Michael walked in. "What in the world are you doing?"

Katie looked at him without saying anything. Finally, she motioned him forward, closing the door behind him to keep their exercise private. She walked him back to the toy table and explained. "I was pretending to be the kidnapper. If Elaine was at this table and struggled with him, I was trying to figure out how he managed to get her out of the room without disturbing any of the other tables. Pretend you are the kidnapper. I'm a bit taller than Elaine, but see if you can carry me out of the room without bumping into anything."

Michael looked at her like she had sprouted another head.

"Come on, Michael. Humor me. Let's assume that Elaine was unconscious after the struggle. If she hadn't been, there is absolutely no way he would have gotten her out of here without more tables being overturned."

Michael just nodded and bent down to pick Katie up. Pulling her over his shoulder in a fireman's carry, he turned and walked toward the door. He hadn't even passed one table before he nearly tripped and landed them both on the floor. Recovering his balance, he moved on. When he finally reached the door, he was sweating and out of breath. Putting her down, he said, "I see what you mean. There's something not right about this. I'm in great shape and that maze was impossible. Our guy has to be in good condition. Let's try something else." Walking back to the toy table, Michael motioned Katie to follow him. Making her lie down on the floor, he grabbed her under the arms and began dragging her toward the door. This, too, proved impossible. The narrow aisles didn't allow for Katie's feet to clear the ends of the tables without dragging them out of their rows.

Michael had almost made it to the door when it opened. A priest stood in the doorway with a confused look in his face. Quickly standing up, Katie was embarrassed to be caught, even though they hadn't been doing anything wrong. Being behind closed doors with a man just felt wrong to her, especially in a church.

"Can I help you?" the priest asked.

"Are you Father Joe?" Michael asked in return.

"Yes, and you are?"

"I'm Special Agent Michael Powell. This is my partner, Special Agent Katie Freeman. We were just walking through the scene of the first disappearance. Do you mind answering a few questions while you're here?"

While Michael went through the standard questions with Father Joe, Katie continued to pace the room. Half listening, she was still running through possible exit paths. It just seemed impossible to get from the back of the room out the only door without disturbing the rest of the yard sale items.

Once Michael asked all the questions he had, Katie wandered into the hall and headed away from the door through which they had entered. With a puzzled look, Michael and Father Joe followed. Further down from the two main rooms, there were a men's and a women's restroom followed by a doorway that led into an office.

"That's my office. Feel free to look around."

Katie merely closed the door and moved on. Across from the office there was a custodial closet and at the end there was a door leading to the altar level of the sanctuary. Continuing through, Katie walked past the confession booths to the left and down the side aisle to the front doors of the church. Opening the doors, she discovered that the church sat right on the street. There was no lot on this side; just the sidewalk that was filled with searchers on their way back in now that darkness had begun to fall. Katie closed the door and began retracing her steps.

Finally realizing that she had an audience, she asked, "Are there any other exit doors to the church?"

Father Joe motioned to the other side of the sanctuary to a door labeled as an exit. Katie went over and opened it only to discover that it opened on the side of the church, but in full view of the parking lot out back. Returning inside, Katie closed the door behind her and the three of them made their way silently back to the other side of the church to see if any of the returning people had found anything.

They entered the room just as a group of three men came forward carrying a purse. Looking inside, the driver's license positively identified it as belonging to Barbie Jones. Also still inside was the small case containing her insulin. Michael met Katie's eyes over the table; both thinking this was not a good sign.

Over the next several hours the remaining searchers returned empty handed, and with no sign of Barbara Jones. The search was stopped for the night and scheduled to pick up at daybreak. At nearly midnight, Katie dragged her tired body into bed to catch a few hours' sleep but thoughts of what Barbie was more than likely going through kept playing in her mind.

CHAPTER SEVEN

Barbie opened her eyes slowly, her mind foggy as she tried to figure out where she was. She tried to swallow and realized there was something metallic in her mouth. She tried to spit it out, but it was somehow attached. Trying to bring her hands to her mouth, she realized that they were tied to the posts on either side of her. Widening her eyes in terror, she frantically looked around. She was standing between two posts in what looked like a cave. The walls were uneven rock and the floor was dirt or clay. Her feet were attached to the bottoms of each post and her arms were stretched above and tied to the tops of the posts. She was also naked. At this thought she began to tremble.

Oh, God where am I? Calm down, Barb, you can figure this out. Why is my brain so foggy? All at once, she felt the sweat streaming down her body; it smelled sickly sweet. She knew what this meant. She had been too long without insulin. She began trying to calm her breathing, knowing the stress would make things worse. So would the sweat. If she dehydrated, she would be even worse off. She had to try to remain calm and think of how to get out of this. This worked until the first strike of something slapped against the naked flesh of her back.

She arched her back and tried to cry out, but the gag in her mouth made it impossible for more than a muted cry to come out. The blows kept raining down over and over and over: on her back, her butt and the backs of her thighs. Barbie had no way to protect herself. She struggled against the ropes holding her in place and kept screaming the useless sounds. After what seemed like forever, the blows stopped.

A figure in a hooded robe walked around her and into her line of vision. She blinked the tears that were streaming from her eyes so she could see him better. The robes were ceremonial priest robes, but the hood didn't belong in any ceremony she had ever seen. A deep voice rasped out, "You killed innocent babies."

Desperately shaking her head, Barbie tried to tell him that she would never kill a baby. She had tried so hard to have one of her own. Thinking of all the miscarriages she had gone through had her crying harder and shaking her head vehemently in denial of his words. This seemed to infuriate him further and the blows from the whip in his hand began raining down on her breasts, stomach and thighs. Barbie's vision began to dim and she knew she was very close to passing out. She tried to stay conscious so she could tell him that someone had misinformed him. That she could never kill an innocent baby. But her body wouldn't hang on any longer and the darkness claimed her.

As her body slumped into unconsciousness, the man paused in his strikes. Thinking she had just passed out from the pain, he reached over and grabbed the ammonia on the table beside the whipping post and waved the vial under her nose. She didn't stir. Frowning, he dropped the whip and used his hand to slap her across the face. When that still didn't revive her, he pinched her left nipple as hard as he could. Still, Barbie didn't stir. Quickly, he cut the ropes holding her up and let her drop to the floor. He put his head against her chest and listened for a heartbeat. Not hearing one, he became angry. *How could she die so soon? She hasn't been punished enough. She should suffer for what she did to those innocent babies.* Striking her again and getting no response, he let her head fall to the floor with a loud *thunk*.

The man began pacing the small space. He had to get her out of there. He couldn't be around a defiler for long. He couldn't be in their deceased presence or their evil might infect him. Needing to know where the searchers were, he slipped out of his robe and climbed the stairs that were dug into the wall. Listening closely for sounds on the other side, he slipped through the panel in the wall and rejoined the crowd in the back room of the church. Ascertaining that the search had ended for the night, the man returned to her lifeless body and scooped it up. Moving quickly, he went down the underground tunnel at the other side of the room and placed the body in the back of his van. Without using lights, he drove to Barbie's home and quickly dumped her body on the porch and drove away.

Chuck lay in the darkness of the trailer clutching Barbie's pillow to his face. He was afraid that if he cried, his tears would wash away her scent. His three dogs lay on the floor beside the bed, none of them sleeping either, as if they were missing her too.

Chief Davidson was in the living room, sleeping on the sofa. He had said he needed to stay close, in case a ransom call came in, but they both knew no ransom call was going to come. The hum of the window air conditioner was the only sound in the quiet night.

Suddenly, Mack, the leader of the pack of dogs came to his feet. The other two quickly followed. None of them made a sound, they all just headed for the front door, but every hair on their bodies stood on end, making the hair on the back of Chuck's neck stand up as well. Quickly grabbing pants, Chuck followed them, knowing from their body language that something was wrong. As they entered the room, the Chief sat straight up, thinking he was about to be attacked. The dogs passed the couch without a second look and went right to the door. Whining, Mack began scratching the front door, trying desperately to get out. Chuck quickly opened the door and nearly fell over the body of his wife laying at his feet. She was completely naked and there were welts all over her body.

"Holy Christ," Chief Davidson said as he grabbed his radio and called for an ambulance.

Chuck dropped to his knees and felt for a pulse. He was entirely calm, though he didn't know why. His entire focus was making sure the love of his life was alive and protecting her as best as he could. Feeling the weak pulse in her throat, he pushed the chief out of his way and barged back into the house. He grabbed the small basket beside the couch and brought it back to Barbie's side. Pulling out a glucose meter, he quickly took her sugar level then returned to the kitchen to get insulin and a needle. Measuring a small dose, he gave Barbie a shot. He had never seen numbers so high, so he wasn't sure exactly how much to give her, but he seemed to recall from somewhere that giving too much - especially if the person were unconscious - was dangerous. He could only pray that he had given her enough to keep her alive long enough for the doctors to stabilize her. Chuck dropped the needle into the basket, knowing Barbie would yell at him later for not disposing of it properly. His hands began to shake just as the sirens from the ambulance broke the night.

CHAPTER EIGHT

The blare of her cell phone woke Katie from a deep sleep at three thirty a.m. "Freeman," she said sleepily.

"Get up, we got a survivor," Michael's tired voice came through the line. "I'm on my way to get you. Be there in ten." He disconnected the phone as her heart began beating faster in her chest.

We have a survivor. What exactly did those words mean? Were there previous victims they didn't know about? Had Barbie been found alive? As Katie pulled on slacks and a long sleeved t-shirt, she became more and more irritated at Michael and at the men in her life. Her boss had yet to contact her to tell her about this case. He had called Michael. The Chief had called Michael about the survivor, even though he had both of their contact information. She was getting really tired of being treated like a tag-along partner. Brushing her teeth and twisting her hair into her traditional bun, she thought, "*As soon as Michael gets here, I'm going to have a few words with him.*"

As Katie quietly snuck down the stairs, carrying her shoes so her sock feet would make less noise, she heard voices from the kitchen. Turning the corner, she entered the room to find Michael sitting at the kitchen table and Caroline wrapping breakfast sandwiches in paper towels.

Smiling at her, Caroline said, "I heard your phone and figured you were about to head out for another long day. When Michael lived here, he was often called out in the middle of the night. Here's some breakfast." She handed over a toasted English muffin with a slice of ham, a scrambled egg and cheese on it. It smelled so good that Katie's mouth watered before she even reached for it.

Katie quickly pulled on her shoes and thanked Caroline for the sandwich. With some of her anger softened by the gesture, Katie merely turned toward the door with a dark look sent to Michael, her mouth too full of food to form the words that she wanted to say. Besides, her brain said, it isn't his fault that the other men are acting like sexist jerks.

Michael quietly got into the driver's seat as he polished off his second sandwich. "Not a morning person, huh?"

"I'm just fine, thank you. I'm just tired of being surrounded by sexists." Katie muttered as she bent down to tie the lace she hadn't tied when rushing to get ready.

"Uh huh."

"What's that supposed to mean?" Katie asked, irritated.

"Well, your one sentence answers seem to indicate that you are not a morning person. And since when did I become a sexist?"

"Since the minute I first saw you," she answered. "Don't think I didn't see you checking me out in the stairwell. Also, you always assume you are driving. I do have a license and know how to operate a motor vehicle, you know." Katie didn't really know where her petulance was coming from; she hated driving. Growing up, there were rarely cars on her mother's property. She certainly had never seen her mom drive one. Of course, her mother never left the property, so why would she need a car? Her mother had Patty and other women from the local shelter to bring her groceries and the essentials from the store. They also brought Katie's schoolbooks and any library books they thought she might enjoy. Shaking herself from thoughts of home, Katie glared over at Michael, but didn't say anything further.

"You're right. I did check you out in the stairwell. But it isn't because you're beautiful. It's because I'm the only one who actually uses those stairs." Michael hoped this lie was believable. He thought she was extremely beautiful and everything male in him had stood at attention when he found her in the stairwell. "I was surprised to find someone else in there. And as for never asking you to drive, I figured it would be faster for me to drive until you found your way around. I was trying to help you out, not be a sexist."

"Why is it that SAC Nelson contacted you to tell you about this case and not me? He has my information, too. If he is really trying to watch me, you would think he would inform me of the cases that come our way. Also, Chief Davidson felt the need to call you when he had my card as well as yours. Is the south always so sexist? I've been down here for a little over two years and Louisiana was just as bad as Tennessee is turning out to be." Her green eyes were flashing as she finished her speech.

Michael just kept his mouth shut as he sped toward Shelbyville. After five minutes of silence and several drinks of coffee later, Katie took a calming breath and finally asked, "So what did you mean when you said we had a survivor? Did they find Barbie, or are there others that got away or were dumped alive?"

"Barbie was dumped on her front porch about fifteen minutes before I called you. She was unconscious, but alive. The husband gave her an insulin shot to stabilize her until the medics could arrive. So far, she is hanging in there. Once the ambulance pulled away, Chief Davidson called me. I called you, and here we are." As he finished, Michael pulled into the parking lot of the small Bedford County Medical Center.   "This is the closest medical facility that's capable of handling a diabetic patient," he explained.

He parked the car and got out. Katie met him at the front of the car and they headed into the hospital. There was a deputy at the door waiting for them. "Right this way," he said and turned right down the hall leading deeper into the emergency department. They stopped outside cubicle three, where both Chief Davidson and Chuck Jones were standing. Chuck kept alternately running his hands through his hair and curling them into fists. He didn't seem to notice that he was bare-chested and his jeans hadn't been buttoned. His feet were crammed into unlaced work boots and the jeans looked like they could use a good wash. The minute Chuck saw the agents he stopped pacing. "Someone just dumped her on the porch. Her little body was covered in welts. What the hell did he do to her?" His voice was an agonized moan. They were the first words he had spoken since finding Barbie on their porch. He immediately broke down into tears and sat on the chair outside the curtain.

Katie turned away, uncomfortable, as Michael squatted down beside Chuck's chair. Gently, Michael asked, "How is she?" Instinctively, he knew that getting Chuck to acknowledge that Barbie was alive, even if she was still unconscious or injured, would help him calm down.

Taking a deep breath, Chuck responded, "She's still unconscious. The doctors took her down for x-rays to see if anything was broken. They're giving her insulin slowly, trying to stabilize her blood sugar without sending her into shock. What did he do to her?" Chuck asked again, in a whisper, his eyes filling with tears that he managed to hold back this time.

"We won't know everything that happened until the doctors have finished examining her," Michael replied, as calmly and quietly as he could. "But we do know that if she had welts, she was likely hit with something like a whip." Chuck's shoulders shook as he once again began sobbing. "Just think about her being here with you, Chuck. She's a survivor. Her diabetes might have saved her life." Michael's words slowed Chuck's tears a bit as the doctor approached them.

"Mr. Jones?" The doctor asked.

"Yes, how is she?" Chuck's voice wavered as he shot to his feet, still looking like he was about to collapse. He unconsciously grabbed Michael's arm and held on as if his life depended on it.

"Mr. Jones, are you aware that your wife is pregnant?" the doctor asked.

Chuck looked at him in stunned silence. Finally he managed to say, "We've been trying for a baby for two years. We've had four miscarriages. Is the baby ok? What will happen to it with her sugar levels being all messed up?"

"Mr. Jones, right now we are more concerned with your wife. We don't want to put her through an x-ray, so we're going to try an MRI. She's been taken down to get it started. It will be a bit longer than an x-ray and I didn't want you to worry. We can do an ultrasound after the MRI, but I don't want you to get your hopes up. The upset with her diabetes could cause several birth defects. It is also possible that the fetus won't or hasn't survived. All I know right now is that the pregnancy test came back positive, but the likelihood of the fetus surviving isn't good. I'm sorry to bring such mixed news. I will let you know as soon as I know more about your wife." The doctor's tone was matter of fact, but held a bit of sympathy. He tried to be as gentle in his delivery as he could, but also had to make sure the husband understood the situation. As the doctor turned to go, Katie touched his arm.

"I'm Special Agent Freeman. This is my partner Special Agent Powell. Would you mind if we walked with you?"

The doctor nodded and headed down the hall trailed by Katie and Michael. "Has Mrs. Jones awakened yet?" Katie asked.

"No, unfortunately she hasn't. It isn't unusual. Her glucose levels are still high. We are slowly getting them leveled out. The longer they're abnormal, the worse the prognosis for the fetus. But I can't worry about that just yet. I am trying to keep her stable and make sure she walks out of here."

"Can you give us any information on her condition other than her glucose levels and the fact that she is pregnant?" Katie persisted.

"I can tell you that she was beaten with something similar to a whip. The narrow lacerations on her torso and legs are proof of that. We'll photograph them once we have her through the MRI. I can also tell you that she wasn't raped. There are ligature marks on her ankles and wrists. The skin is abraded and quite raw. Oh, and we removed the ropes from her wrists and ankles when she came in. Having worked a forensics rotation, I made sure to leave the knots intact and have bagged them as evidence. They are currently secured in the hospital security office. You can sign for them there. I checked her hands for defensive wounds when she was brought in, but there were none. Under her nails was clean, no trace of anything. I don't mean to cut this short, but that is all I know at the present moment. I really do need to check on the other patients while I wait for Mrs. Jones to be brought back from the MRI."

Katie and Michael thanked the doctor and returned to Chuck and Chief Davidson. They asked the Chief a few more questions and then stepped aside to discuss where things stood.

"I feel like we're a step behind on this case," Michael said.

"I agree," replied Katie. "I think we need to go back to the beginning. We need to start as if we were called in when Elaine Henderson was taken. So far, we've only spoken to Rick Henderson. Let's go back and talk to the twin, Evelyn. I think we should also get Dr. Bennett's findings. Perhaps there's something there that will help us. Father Joe might be worth another conversation, but I think we should reserve that for when we have a clearer picture. There's still something bothering me about that church."

"I agree. I also think we should begin looking for anyone in the park yesterday that might have seen Barbie Jones. And we should see if there are any other employees of the church and whether or not they were there when Elaine Henderson disappeared," Michael added.

Checking her watch, Katie nodded. "It's after eight. Let's start the rounds. We can have Chief Davidson call us if or when Barbie wakes up."

Following up with Chief Davidson and getting his assurance that he would notify them immediately with any change in Barbie's condition and that he would wait to ask or answer questions until they arrived, Katie and Michael left the hospital.

CHAPTER NINE

"Where to first?" Michael asked.

"Let's start with Evelyn Baker. She was one of the last people to see her sister alive."

Michael started the car and headed in the direction of the address in the file. Fifteen minutes later he pulled up to the curb in front of a craftsman style house in one of the oldest sections of Shelbyville. The sidewalk was cracked, but otherwise the street was in good condition. All the yards were mowed and the shrubbery was trimmed back with blooming flowers of varying shades of red and pink up and down the street. The woman who answered the door was so similar to the one they had witnessed on the autopsy table that both Michael and Katie took a shocked breath before being able to introduce themselves.

Evelyn's eyes were red and puffy. After identifying themselves, she opened the door and invited them in. As they went in, Katie noted the differences between Elaine and her sister. Evelyn was taller and a little heavier. Her blonde hair was cut short, where Elaine's had been past her shoulders. Her house was very clean and there were religious trinkets on nearly every surface. They were shown into a comfortable and homey living room that had toys strewn across the floor. As they were about to sit, two children came flying down the stairs. "Can we play outside?" the girl asked. Receiving a nod from their aunt, the little girl took her brother's hand and they vanished out the front door.

"Those are Elaine's kids, Austin and Emma. She will never see them grow up." Evelyn broke down crying. It took her a few minutes to collect herself. The agents sat silently waiting, allowing her to grieve.

Katie looked at Michael and gave a small nod, signaling to him that she was okay if he took the lead in questioning Evelyn.

"Are you up to answering a few questions, Ms. Baker?"

"I don't know what more I can tell you than I told Chief Davidson when Elaine disappeared."

"Why don't you just start at the beginning and walk me through the evening."

"We all get together about seven and start planning whatever we are working toward. That night we were putting prices on all the donated items. Elaine rushed in late, as usual. She was always running late, but we didn't mind. She had two kids and a husband to get fed. We worked for about an hour and Elaine left as usual to go talk to Father Joe. She was gone for about fifteen minutes and was a bit distracted when she came back. But again that was normal. I know I am always distracted when I bare my soul to Father Joe. It's just uncomfortable sometimes to think that one man knows all the secrets of this town. I bet if someone farts, he knows who did it. And not because someone would tattle, but because that person would confess it. I know Father Joe can't be much older than me, but he is a gentle, old soul. He is very easy to talk to." The admiration in Evelyn's voice was clear. Katie wondered how deep the woman's feelings for the priest went, and if they were returned.

Katie was fidgeting in her chair, though Michael couldn't figure out why. Perhaps it was because Evelyn was rambling. He shot her a look to try and calm her down, knowing that people in grief needed to tell their story in their own way and in their own time. Just as his eyes met hers, she asked, "So, Ms. Baker, as far as you know, Rick came home from work, they sat down to a family dinner and then Elaine came to the church?"

"Oh, yes. Elaine always made sure that we knew that Rick did the clean up on those nights. He was so supportive of her and the kids."

Katie merely nodded. Michael looked at her confused, but when she didn't follow up with another question, he turned back to Evelyn and said, "Please continue."

"Where was I? Oh, yes, her confession. Well, we worked on and each of the women took their turn going up to confession. Once the last of us had had our turn, we always had what we call comedy hour. We all laughed and joked and did our best to make sure it was a relaxing evening. I mean, how often do we all get to be together without husbands and children? Of course that didn't apply to me. I'm happy being an old maid. I have my sister's kids all the time, though. And Mondays were our special night. Elaine would bring them over so Rick could have one quiet evening. She usually went to the library or ran errands or some such thing. Me and the kids would play and read and work in the yard or garden." Her eyes welled with tears and she took a few more minutes to gather herself. "I sure hope Rick allows me to keep them close. They are my only link to her now."

Katie was surprised to hear Evelyn call herself an old maid. She was only in her mid-thirties. But she kept her mouth closed as she exchanged a look with Michael. Something more was going on, she just didn't know what yet. "Ms. Baker, what happened after comedy hour that night?"

"Well, we worked a bit later than normal. We have so many donations this year." She smiled sadly at this. "It was about 10:15 when we left. Elaine walked me to my car, even though it was three spots down from hers. She waited until I was inside and then I watched as she went to her car. She was taking a long time to get in, so I rolled my window down to see what was taking so long. She said she couldn't find her keys and was going to run back inside before Father locked up for the night. I told her I could just take her home, no need to disturb Father if he was still working. But she just waved me off and went back inside. Father Joe came out a few minutes later and came over to talk to me. We talked for, I don't know, maybe ten minutes. Finally I mentioned how long it was taking and that we should go help her look so all of us could get some sleep. We went inside and there was her purse on the table by the door. We looked into the yard sale room and saw the mess with the toy table. I went to the ladies room to see if she was there and Father Joe went into the sanctuary. Neither of us found her. We went room to room, but she wasn't there. The front and side doors were already locked for the night, so the only way she could have gone back out was the back door. I looked outside to see if maybe we had crossed paths while we were searching. She wasn't outside. Father called the police. I told all this to the police the night Elaine went missing." Taking a deep breath, Evelyn looked at the two agents. "What could I have done differently? Could I have saved her?"

Michael reached over and took her hand. "There was nothing you could have done to stop this. This happened because there is a very sick individual out there who is taking advantage of women." Waiting a beat, Michael then asked, "Evelyn, was there any time during your search of the church that Father Joe was out of your sight for a period of time?"

"You can't think he did this? Surely not! There is just no way." Seeing their silent, serious faces, Evelyn knew they considered Father Joe a suspect. "I don't believe it. He couldn't... He wasn't out of my sight for more than a few seconds. I peeked in the bathroom and then met him in the main sanctuary. We thought she might have checked for her keys in the confessional. He was looking in there when I went in. We walked up and down the aisles together. We were together practically the whole time. We certainly weren't apart long enough for him to retrieve her from somewhere and move her. There's no way Father Joe did this." Her mulish expression showed that she would never believe anything bad of Father Joe.

Michael asked a few more questions and then the two of them stood and made their way out of the house. They waved to the kids in the yard and got in the car. Turning over the ignition and blasting the air conditioning into the furnace-like interior, Michael turned to Katie without making a move to drive off. "I can tell you caught something. I don't know what Evelyn said that got you excited, but something is going on in that brain of yours."

Katie gave a smug smile, knowing she had picked up on something he hadn't. "Evelyn said Elaine was always late, rushing in at the last minute to get started at these meetings. Rick said that Elaine left the house by five; that they ate without her on Wednesday nights. Where did Elaine go every Wednesday between five and seven? Also, is it the same place as she went on Mondays while Evelyn kept the kids? It would be worth a trip to the library to see if she even had a library card. I think Elaine had something going on that her family didn't know about."

"Hmm, maybe something that ties her to Barbie Jones. They had to have more in common than blonde hair and church volunteer work." Michael finally put the car in gear and headed toward the public library.

Walking up to the front counter, Michael and Katie flashed their identification to the elderly woman sitting behind the desk.

"Oh, you must be here about poor Elaine and Barbie. Those poor dears. I do hope Barbie is going to be ok?" She looked up expectantly.

"I'm sorry, but we cannot comment on her condition," Katie stated bluntly.

Michael jumped in with a softer tone. "I'm sure the doctors are doing everything they possibly can." He flashed her a megawatt smile as he leaned on the counter. Katie could see her melt right in front of them. She wanted to roll her eyes, but knew better than to alienate the woman. They needed information.

Michael continued to smile as he asked, "Can you tell me if either of them were patrons of the library?"

"Oh, yes. They both were. Elaine was here for reading time every Monday." Katie felt her heart sink in disappointment. She had been so sure that Elaine was up to something. Then the librarian continued, "Reading time was from ten a.m. until noon. The elementary kids would come across the street and they would hear a story for an hour and then roam around looking for books to check out for another hour. She would always help them find something they were interested in. Now, Barbie, she was here every Thursday. She would take our arts and crafts classes. We have classes on everything from painting to sewing to cooking. We have a room in the back that is equipped for just about anything you could teach."

Katie was nearly coming out of her skin by the time the woman finished talking. She and Michael bid the woman farewell and headed back to the car. As Michael was buckling his seatbelt, Katie said, "I knew it! Elaine was up to something. Let's go have another chat with the husband."

Unfortunately, that chat was postponed as Michael's phone rang. Seeing the number for Chief Davidson, he handed the phone to Katie to answer. He figured it would appease her to be able to get some news firsthand.

"Special Agent Freeman," she answered.

"Oh, I thought I called Agent Powell," the chief stuttered.

"You did. But, as I am just as capable of answering a phone, he passed his to me." Katie just smiled, even though the chief couldn't see her.

"Um, well, you guys asked me to call if there was a change. Barbie woke up a few minutes ago. The doctor is with her now, but she is asking all kinds o' questions. You want me to tell her something specific?" Chief Davidson stuttered his way through the statement.

"No, we're on our way. We'll be there in five."

Turning to Michael, she relayed the information. He immediately turned the car toward the hospital. "You enjoyed that, didn't you?"

Still smiling and with green eyes sparkling mischievously, she said, "Of course. I get tired of being treated unfairly because of my gender."

"You know, you owe me two facts about yourself. You didn't give me one yesterday and you haven't given me one yet today."

Katie's smile evaporated. She sat quietly for a few minutes. Finally, she turned and said, "I don't like hospitals. I was only in one once as a kid, when I had to have my tonsils removed. There are your two facts." She sat back in the seat and looked out the windshield.

"That's only one fact. You hate hospitals. Everyone hates hospitals."

"Actually that was two facts. One, I hate hospitals and two, I had my tonsils removed." She smiled angelically at him.

"I think that's cheating. You haven't told me anything, really." Katie just laughed as she got out of the car in the hospital parking lot.

The both sobered as they neared Barbie's room. Neither was looking forward to this discussion. They got to the room as the doctor came out to talk with Chuck.

"She's stable for now," the doctor began. "Per your request, we didn't mention the pregnancy. She seems a little confused, which is to be expected until her glucose levels stabilize. Some of what happened may come back, or it may not. It really depends on how much she was conscious for."

"May we talk to her?" Katie asked.

"With her family's consent, I don't see why not. Just keep in mind that she is groggy and needs to avoid as much stress as possible. It won't do her body or the fetus any good to endure more stress than they already have."

"Please don't call our baby a fetus," Chuck said. "We have tried for so long to get pregnant that any baby is a blessing. It seems wrong to use that word." His words were spoken softly. It was plain that it cost him emotionally to think of another baby that probably wouldn't survive, this time due to unfathomable circumstances. Chuck turned to the agents, "You can go in and talk to her, but I'm going in with you. If I think she's getting upset at all, I will ask you to leave. Clear?" Chuck had gone into super-protective husband mode. He waited for them to agree and then led the way into Barbie's room, Chief Davidson bringing up the rear.

Barbie lay in the bed staring blankly out the window, her small frame covered by the sheet making her look even smaller. Most of the machines she had been hooked to earlier had been taken away. All that remained was an IV bag hanging from a pole to her left. Approaching the bed, Chuck reached out and took his wife's hand gently in his. Barbie turned her head and looked up at him. Chuck leaned down and kissed her on the lips. "I love you, beautiful," he said. Barbie's eyes filled with tears that overflowed down her cheeks.

"I love you too, handsome," she replied. "I thought I would never see you again." She wrapped her arms around Chuck's neck and hung on with a strength that belied her small stature.

"I wouldn't let that happen. I would have torn apart every inch of this state to find you." They looked into each other's eyes for several minutes, as if they were having a private conversation. Finally, Chuck said, "There are two FBI agents here to talk to you. Do you feel up to it?"

Barbie turned and looked at the two agents standing at the foot of her bed. "I'll try to answer your questions. I'm a bit fuzzy about things though."

Michael moved to the other side of the bed and sat in the chair so he wouldn't tower over her. Katie remained at the foot of the bed, watching her reactions. They introduced themselves and Michael began by asking, "Can you take us through the steps of your day?"

"Well, I was off work yesterday. It was yesterday right?" At the nod from all four of them, Barbie relaxed a bit and continued. "I work part time at the grocery, but it was my day off. See, Chuck and I, we decided that me working part time would be best. It helps me relax and maybe we can get pregnant sooner." She squeezed his hand, assuming the tears in his eyes were for their past babies, not suspecting there was more to it. "Anyway, I loaded up the stuff to take to the church. David was there when I got there and he helped me unload the stuff."

"Who's David?" Katie asked. The other four turned to look at her. It was Chuck who answered.

"David is the guy who helps around the church. I guess you would call him the handyman, but he does lots of stuff. He fixes the plumbing, takes out the trash, and cleans up after services. You know, just general stuff."

"Ok, please continue," Michael said, bringing attention back to the events of the day and filing away the name for future consideration. It was interesting that no one had mentioned his name before. He didn't even recall it being in the case file.

"Well, we got everything in the church and David gave me a drink of water. It was so hot that day and I was thirsty. I felt a little shaky. I even debated not going to the park; I thought I might need to get home and eat something. But I rested a few minutes and talked with David and Father Joe." She paused and rolled her eyes with a small laugh. "Father Joe scolded me for not coming to confession lately, so we went to the sanctuary and into the confessional. I joked with him that I was perfectly fine giving my confession in the back room of the church, that I didn't need a sacred space, but Father Joe likes the tradition. Could I get a drink of water, please?" Chuck immediately stood and poured her a drink from the pitcher beside the bed. After a few drinks and even more deep breaths, Barbie continued with her story.

"I left the church and went over to the park. It was so hot that there weren't many kids out. Probably more the moms who can't take the heat than the kids wanting to stay inside. I remember little Petey Walker and his mom were there. We talked for about thirty minutes. The heat was sapping my energy, so I got up to go back to my car. I knew I needed to get into the air conditioning and get home to eat. That's all I remember, before..." Barbie's body began to tremble at this point and Chuck gently wrapped his arms around her.

"You don't have to say another word, if you don't want to. You just focus on you and keeping yourself healthy."

"Chuck, you know I can't do that. There's someone out there kidnapping people like poor Elaine and me. Has there been any word on her?"

Chuck stiffened and laid her back on the bed. He looked over his shoulder at Michael, imploring him to answer that question.

"Elaine was found yesterday morning. She didn't make it," was all Michael said. Barbie began to cry and Chuck gently rocked her back and forth. Everyone stood silently as Barbie let out her grief for her friend. Finally, she pulled herself together.

"Do you think it was the same man that did this to me? Was he gonna kill me too?" Her words were quiet, but there was the underlying strength behind them that Katie had seen in the picture of her with the dead deer.

It was Katie who answered. She knew that Barbie could handle more than the men thought she was capable of. "Yes, we think it was the same person. We also think that your diabetes saved your life. If you hadn't gone into shock and lost consciousness, there is no doubt that person would still have you."

Michael was about to say something to soften Katie's words, but Barbie's nod and simple thank you stopped him. The men stood silently as the women gazed at each other, taking measure of the other's strength.

Finally, Barbie continued, "The first thing I remember is that I was underground. The walls were not smooth. They looked like rock, like someone had dug this room in the ground, but not finished it. Kind of like a cellar or something. The floor was dirt, or packed clay. Of course, this is Tennessee and there isn't much difference between dirt and clay around here. There were two pillars in the middle of the room and I was tied to them." Chuck gasped and looked away. Barbie squeezed his hand and when he looked at her she said, "You don't have to stay and listen if you don't want to. I'm okay."

Chuck just shook his head. "I'm not leaving you to go through this alone again. I am always gonna be right beside you." He brought her hand to his lips and kissed the back of it. Laying their joined hands back down, he encouraged her to continue.

"My feet were tied to the bottom and my hands to the top. Like I was a giant X. I was seeing black dots right away, so I knew I had been there for a while. I was so thirsty, but my tongue wouldn't move. Then I realized that there was something in my mouth. It was metallic and there was a band that went around my head to keep it in. It muffled any sound I made and it hurt my teeth." She unconsciously licked her lips and ran her tongue along the inside of her teeth. "I think some of my teeth might be chipped." Barbie caught the look that passed between Michael and Katie. "What? Is that important?" she asked.

Again, it was Katie who answered. "It does reinforce the connection between your abduction and Elaine's. She had signs of biting something hard as well."

Barbie nodded and went on, "I realized I was naked right about then. But I kept talking to myself. I was trying to keep myself calm. I knew that if I got too stressed it wouldn't be good, especially because I didn't have access to my insulin. I was trying to look around and figure out how to get out of the ropes when the first strike came." Chuck involuntarily squeezed her hand. He was trying so hard to remain impassive, but hearing what his wife had gone through was his undoing. Tears began to roll down his cheeks as she continued to tell what had happened.

When she finished her story, Katie asked, "Did he ever speak to you?"

Barbie thought for a few minutes, replaying the events in her mind. "Yes, he did," she said excitedly. "He said that I had murdered innocent babies and that I had to be punished. I tried to tell him that he had been misinformed, but the thing in my mouth wouldn't let me speak. I just shook my head trying to let him know that I could never hurt a baby." As she spoke these words, she began to cry again and Chuck got up to gather her in his arms once more. He sent the agents a look that let them know the interview was over for the time being.

Patting Barbie's leg as she stood, Katie motioned to Michael that it was time to leave. They made their way from the room, telling Chief Davidson they would come back if they had further questions.

Katie and Michael made their way out of the hospital and back to the car. Neither of them said anything as they processed Barbie's story. Once the air conditioning had cooled the car, Michael looked over and asked, "What do you think?"

She paused before answering. "I think we really didn't learn anything useful. We already knew he used an iron gag and that he whipped them. She couldn't give a clear idea of how she was taken or where the lair was. Let's give her a bit of time to calm down while we go back and talk to Rick Henderson. When we come back, I want to know what Barbie did on Monday nights. Perhaps there is a connection there."

Michael nodded and turned the car in the direction of the Henderson's home.

As they drove off, Michael said, "You were really good with her."

Katie smiled at the compliment. "I just understood her. I knew she had more strength than you or Chuck were giving her credit for. She needed someone to be straight with her and not soft-pedal the news. Her mind would have made the scenario worse if we had told her partial truths in there. How about we try Rick Henderson now?"

Michael knew she needed to move on, that she wasn't used to compliments. "How about we get some lunch first?" It was after one in the afternoon and neither had eaten since 3:30 this morning. Katie nodded and Michael pulled out of the hospital lot.

A few minutes later, Michael pulled into the drive thru of a fast food restaurant. "Surely we aren't eating here!" Katie exclaimed.

"What's wrong with this place? It's an American tradition. We all grew up on these burgers."

"Not me," Katie said. "I have never eaten here. In fact, I've never been through a drive thru."

Michael looked at her as if she had three heads. "How can you be twenty-six years old and never been through a drive thru? I thought you said you grew up in Arizona, not on Mars. I know they have fast food in Arizona."

Katie bit her lip. She had never told anyone about how she grew up. It was her secret. She already felt like an outcast when it came to pop culture, so she always avoided conversations that involved her childhood. She knew she wouldn't get out of this as easily. "My mother was a stickler about nutrition. We grew our own vegetables and canned or froze them for the winter. We had meat delivered from nearby farms. Most of the time, we traded vegetables for the meat." It was the best that Katie could do without revealing too much.

Michael seemed to accept the information, but he wasn't letting her off the hook about the drive thru, or the food. "Well, today, I'm treating you to your first fine dining experience!" He wiggled his eyebrows as he shot her a grin that would make any woman's heart pound. Katie wanted to think she was immune, but her body responded as her heart picked up its pace. He pulled up to the speaker and ordered from the menu. Katie didn't understand a thing coming from the speaker, but apparently Michael had no trouble at all.

As they pulled to the first window and Michael paid for their lunch, Katie just sat in the seat and looked around as if she expected to be struck by lightning being caught in a drive thru line.

Once he had collected their food from the second window, Michael pulled the car into a parking space and began dishing out the fries and burgers. He sat the drinks in the cup holder between them. Katie opened the cardboard box containing her sandwich and looked at the lettuce and sauce oozing from between the two patties of meat and the bun. Picking it up and taking a bite, she tried hard to conceal the moan that wanted to escape as the flavor hit her tongue. There was no way she would give Michael the satisfaction of knowing that it was the best burger she had ever tasted. Apparently she wasn't as good an actress as she wanted to be.

Michael chuckled and gave her a satisfied smile as he bit into his own burger and used a fry to swipe some of the sauce from the inside of the container. Following his lead, Katie picked up a fry and gathered up the extra sauce. This time she couldn't stop the sigh that escaped. This made Michael laugh even harder. Michael had gotten her a sweet tea to go with the meal. "How did you know I drank sweet tea?"

"I *am* a trained investigator," was his reply. He just smiled as they finished their meals in a comfortable silence and tossed the wrappers in the trash bin beside the building.

CHAPTER TEN

They found the Henderson home overflowing with people. As they approached the front door, an elderly man came down the sidewalk, looking angry. "We ain't got no use for you damn reporters. Now you just turn your sorry behinds around and git off this property."

Michael pulled his credentials from his pocket and identified himself to the man.

"Hmpf," the man grunted. "Fine, come on in. You didn't bother to show up in time to help my little girl. Don't know what you can do now to make this right. I'm Harold Baker, Lainie's dad." At this admission, the man seemed to age another ten years; his skin had already gone slack and turned an unhealthy grey. What little hair he had left was combed neatly to his scalp, but his eyes were the same blue as both his daughters. He couldn't seem to stop the tears that flowed down his cheeks. "Something mighty wrong with a man havin' to bury his youngun. Mighty wrong, indeed."

Michael and Katie exchanged a glance as they followed Mr. Baker into the house. They found Rick Henderson slumped on the couch as the other people milled around. Occasionally, an elderly woman would nudge him and make him eat a bite or take a drink of water.

"Mr. Henderson, might we have a word with you in private?" Michael asked as he slowly approached the man. The room went instantly silent, all heads turning in the direction of the agents.

"I ain't got nothing to hide," Rick said, his words slightly slurred.

"He had a few beers before we got here," the elderly woman said. "I'm Rick's mom, Heidi. I've been trying to get him to drink some water. The kids are coming home tonight. I don't want them to see their dad drunk when we already have to tell them their mom isn't ever coming home." Heidi teared up as she spoke.

"Have you found who killed my wife?" Rick asked. He was beginning to get belligerent, though the sob that broke through at the end of his question showed he was trying to hide the pain.

"No, I'm sorry, we haven't found him yet. But we would like to ask a few more questions, if we may," Michael replied. Michael helped Rick off the sofa and the two of them made their way to the office at the back of the house, with Katie trailing behind.

Once the door was closed behind them and Rick had lowered himself into one of the chairs, Michael asked, "Can you tell us about Elaine's week, Monday through Sunday? We need to know in detail what she did, so we can look for similarities to the abduction of Barbara Jones."

Rick just shook his head sadly. "You know, I thought we were as close as a couple could be, but I really don't know what she did all week. I know Mondays were the library reading day and Monday nights she spent with her sister and the kids. I had a standing poker night with some guys from church. Tuesdays were her in-service school days. She would go to the school and help out in either Austin's or Emma's classroom. Wednesdays she did the grocery shopping and made dinner so it was ready to just be reheated for the kids. Then she would head out to the church. The other nights we stayed home as a family. I assume she spent the other days cleaning and stuff around here. Saturdays we went to the kids' games or recitals, and Sundays we went to church and out to lunch. There wasn't anything that stands out. I know there were a few days a month that she volunteered at the women's shelter and at a dog rescue place. That's about it. She liked to keep busy, but wasn't overcommitted so that she could always be around for anything the kids needed. All she ever wanted was to be a mom." Rick looked up at them with red-rimmed, anguished eyes. "Why did he kill my wife, but let Barbie Jones live?"

Katie and Michael looked at each other, not really sure how much to reveal. Finally, Katie said, "Barbie Jones is diabetic. She became unconscious because she didn't have access to her insulin. We don't know why he let her go, but it is likely he panicked."

Rick just put his head in his hands and sighed. All the life seemed to drain out of him as he absorbed one more blow. His wife had been healthy and strong and as a result she had died.

"Rick, I need to ask you something difficult," Michael began. "We talked to Evelyn earlier about Elaine's schedule. She mentioned that on Mondays Elaine dropped the kids off and then went back out. She claimed that Elaine went to the library or ran various errands that she didn't have time to do other times during the week. What do you think she did during these hours?"

Rick looked up with wide eyes. "I thought she went over and spent time with her sister. Are you telling me she wasn't there? She was supposed to be there!" It was apparent that Rick had no clue his wife had been anything but honest and straightforward.

"One more question. When she left here on Wednesdays, she went straight to the church?" Michael asked. At Rick's nod, he followed up, "And she left here at five?" Again Rick nodded.

"Why do you ask?" It hurt Rick to ask the question. His confusion warred with curiosity and fear.

"Well, the ladies at church said that Elaine was always late. That she came rushing in right at seven or a few minutes after. We were just wondering why it took her two hours to drive ten minutes down the road." Michael left the thought hanging, hoping that Rick would reveal something.

"There is no way my wife was having an affair," Rick declared. He was adamant that this could not happen. "I would have known if she was having an affair. She was never unfaithful. We're Catholic, for crying out loud."

Michael just nodded and thanked Rick for his time, finding it interesting that Rick's thoughts immediately jumped to an affair. Promising to find out the truth and to keep Rick updated with progress, the agents left the house.

"Where to next?" Michael asked Katie as they buckled their seatbelts.

"I think we need to go back and talk to Father Joe and also find out who this David character is. I find it interesting that he's never mentioned in the police report of Elaine's disappearance."

Michael pulled a U-turn in the middle of the residential street and headed back toward Christ the King Church.

Pulling into the parking lot behind the church, Katie and Michael saw Father Joe tossing garbage bags into the dumpster at the back of the lot. "Evening, agents, what can I do for you tonight?" Father Joe said as he wiped his hands on his trousers.

"Didn't peg you for one to take out the trash, Father," Katie observed.

"Well, David didn't show up today, so someone has to do it. We are a small parish, so that falls to me."

Katie's antennae perked up at this information. "What is David's last name?" she asked calmly.

"Williams," the Father replied. "Why?"

"We just find it odd that he was never mentioned in the report filed on Elaine's disappearance. You would think that all employees of the church would have been interviewed," Katie replied. Michael stood back and let Katie take the lead. This was a circumstance that required directness, not finesse.

"Well, David wasn't around that day. Wednesdays he takes off and goes, well wherever he goes on his day off," Father Joe said. "He seems to have had a difficult life, though he doesn't talk much. He just does his job and doesn't bother anyone."

"What exactly is his job?"

"He does all the chores around this place. Mows the lawn, does the landscaping, cleans the facilities, takes out the trash, moves anything heavy. He usually set up the room for the ladies on Tuesday nights so it was ready when they gathered on Wednesdays."

Katie paused a minute. "So he would have known Elaine and Barbie?"

"Of course. He would have seen them at mass or any other time they came into the church." Father Joe was beginning to get indignant. "Don't go trying to blame this on him. He's a gentle soul, wouldn't hurt a flea."

Michael stepped in, "We are still looking at everyone. We just thought it odd that he wasn't mentioned in the police report. It makes sense now if he wasn't around that night." Glancing at Katie, he saw the daggers she was shooting his way. He just raised his eyebrows and turned back to Father Joe. "Can you tell us what Elaine confessed to you on the Wednesday she disappeared?"

"Now young man, you know confessions are privileged information." All the calmness Father Joe had disappeared at the question.

Katie smirked at Michael. Even she knew that question was out of line. Katie hadn't been raised with any formal religion, but she had read enough on the subject to know Catholics took their traditions seriously. She decided it was once again her turn to ask the questions.

"Father, since you cannot break that confidentiality, might I run a theory by you?" She waited for his acknowledgement before continuing.

"Let's say a respected wife and mother was becoming bored with her life. She was in her mid-thirties with two young elementary-aged children, a husband that worked and provided for the family, and not enough to occupy her time now that the kids were in school. Let's say that her dreams of being a mother and housewife were not living up to expectations. So she began to look elsewhere for something to fulfill her. She had two nights a week to go out and be free. She meets a man, one thing leads to another, and she's involved before she knows it." Katie paused to gauge Father Joe's reaction.

"That is an interesting story, but I'm afraid I can neither confirm nor deny its correctness. Elaine was a wonderful woman who loved her family with all that she had. She was a good Catholic." That was as much as Father Joe was going to say on the subject. He didn't directly dismiss the idea, though.

"Father, you do realize that if Elaine Henderson was having an affair, it could be what got her killed?" Katie said in exasperation.

Father Joe fired right back, "What would be the connection then between Elaine and Barbie? Barbie is as innocent as the driven snow. She didn't deserve this." His anger revealed more than he intended.

"So you're saying that Elaine had an affair, but Barbie didn't." Katie returned. "Interesting."

"You are putting words in my mouth, young lady," Father Joe said. "Do you have any other questions?"

"No, that's all for now. Thanks for your help." Katie smiled angelically as she turned and headed back to the car. Michael just shook his head and followed, mumbling under his breath about headstrong women and the need to always be right.

By the time Michael got in the car, Katie was dialing the phone. "Who are you calling?" he asked. Katie just smiled as she waited for the person on the other end to pick up.

"Lucy, it's Katie Freeman. We met in the break room the other day? I was wondering if you could do me a favor?" She paused as Lucy responded. "Great, I need you to look up a man named David Williams. He currently works for Christ the King Church in Shelbyville, but that's all we know about him." Katie just "mmm'd" and "uh huh'd" for the next few minutes before thanking Lucy and hanging up.

Michael just shook his head and turned the car toward home.

CHAPTER ELEVEN

The Bed & Breakfast was full of life and laughter when Katie and Michael walked in. Kevin was standing at the sink cleaning up the supper dishes while Caroline stood folding a load of towels. Ten-year-old Ian was sitting at the table working on homework, his brow creased in concentration.

"What's a cellar?" Ian asked.

"Well, it's..."Caroline began.

"It's a basement," Michael cut in, grinning as a chorus of "Uncle Michael!" rang out from all three kids. They crowded around Michael as he walked through the door. He hugged the boys and swung little Carrie up into his arms, planting a loud smacking kiss on her cheek as she screamed out a laugh. Placing Carrie back on the floor, Michael leaned over and kissed his sister's cheek and shook hands with his brother-in-law. "I sure hope you saved some dinner. It smells wonderful," Michael said with a longing glance at the refrigerator.

"You know I did. I figured you two would be much later than this. Have you already wrapped up your case?" Caroline started pulling covered dishes from the refrigerator and warmed them in the microwave.

"No, we haven't even had a break in the case," Katie said as she sat in the seat Caroline waved her toward. Katie's mouth was watering at the smell of the food. She knew without asking that Caroline had made meatloaf and mashed potatoes. This was confirmed as Caroline placed the plate in front of her. There were also green beans and cornbread. "This was my favorite meal that my mom used to make. She used to call it the free man's meal," Katie offered, as she picked up her fork and dug in.

Michael looked over in surprise. "This is a southern meal. I thought you grew up in Arizona?"

"I did, but I don't think my mom is from there. Come to think of it, she has a slight southern accent. Hmm, I never put that together until now."

"You don't know where your mom is from?" Ian asked. "We did a family tree at the beginning of the school year and I had to learn just about everything for hundreds of years about my family. What did you ever put on your family tree when you did one in school?"

"I didn't go to school," Katie replied. Seeing the shock on his face and the horrified look Kevin and Caroline directed toward her, Katie hurriedly said, "I had to go to school at home. My mother taught me right in our kitchen. I think it was much harder than actually going to school. Can you imagine your mom being your teacher?"

Ian looked aghast as he thought this over. "You mean you never left your house?"

Katie sighed inwardly. She never talked about herself and now she had opened the door for questions. She knew Michael was listening closely, as his fork had stopped moving toward his mouth and was suspended in mid-air. "Well, I left the house, but never the property. See, my mom had about the same size property you have here, but she had walls around hers, not fences. We spent the morning out in the garden, planting or weeding or harvesting. When it was really hot in the afternoons, we would spend it indoors doing my schoolwork. In the evenings, I had to do my chores, like clean my room or do the dishes."

"What about your friends? When did you see them? Didn't you get to play? And what about TV?" Little Tommy's eyes were huge as he asked all these questions.

Katie just laughed. "Well, we didn't have a TV, so I never watched any. I only had friends when we had people staying with us. See, my mom helped women from the local women's shelter. If they needed a place to stay, they could stay with us for however long they needed, as long as they followed the rules. Some stayed a few days and others stayed years. Sometimes they had daughters that came with them. I had a playground and there was a small lake we could swim in. It wasn't so bad." She smiled at Tommy and Ian as they both still looked horrified.

"Man, no TV, I bet you didn't even have a Nintendo." Ian shook his head in disbelief. The adults just laughed.

Seeing that Tommy was about to ask more questions and knowing Katie really didn't want to answer anything more, Michael quickly asked, "So, Ian, why did you need to know about a cellar?" Katie shot him a grateful look as they both resumed eating.

"I'm working on this report for school. I have to research the Underground Railroad. Some of the stuff says that cellars were used, but I didn't know what a cellar was. Why didn't they just say basement?" Ian asked with a disgruntled tone.

Katie tuned out the conversation as her thoughts remained in the past. Her heart ached to see her mother again. The one rule her mother had for the women who came onto the ranch, as it was called, was that they never brought a man, or allowed one to enter. Sarah Freeman had been firm in her belief that her daughter never be exposed to the "evils of man," and she had made sure that Katie was sheltered from anything Sarah deemed to risky. The one person who ever defied that logic was Patty Harris.

Patty had come to the ranch before Katie was born and had never left. A deep friendship had formed between Sarah and Patty, though they were as different as night and day. Sarah had long dark hair, or at least she had when Katie left eight years ago. She also had the big green eyes that Katie had inherited. Patty had short blonde hair, light brown, almost golden eyes, and a more pragmatic approach to life. Patty thought Katie should know what to expect from the world, whereas Sarah though she should be protected from it. Patty was the only woman allowed to come and go from the ranch without question. She would make runs into town and barter for the things that the ranch needed. Patty also registered Katie for homeschooling and renewed licenses or paid taxes, basically anything that needed to be done but couldn't be accomplished from within the walls. She also went to the library and brought back books for Katie. As more and more things began to be put online, she argued with Sarah that Katie should be allowed to learn as much as she could. That was how Katie ended up graduating high school at sixteen and nearly completing a bachelor's degree online by eighteen.

The only fight Katie ever witnessed between her mom and Patty was when Katie announced that she was leaving the ranch. Katie wanted to go to college and experience all the things she had read about. And Katie had read plenty. She was secretly hooked on romance novels, though she also devoured anything having to do with history or crime and punishment. Katie had watched how her mother had run the ranch and knew there was no leniency for any offense. If one of the women returned to their abusive situation or allowed a man to come to the ranch even just as far as the front gate, that woman was escorted out. Mostly, the women stayed long enough to heal from their physical wounds and left, taking their children with them.

It wasn't until Katie read Peter Pan that she found out that men were once boys. She tried once to talk to her mother about why none of the women who came to the ranch had boys, but her mother refused to answer. It was Patty who later explained that Sarah had been hurt in her past and that she didn't want boys or men around. She explained that Sarah was trying to protect Katie. But as Katie grew up and her world expanded through books, her longing to get out and experience life grew as well.

On her eighteenth birthday, Katie registered for the upcoming semester at Arizona State. It was close to home but still far enough away to have some freedom. There were two months until the fall semester started when she told her mother that she would be leaving. Sarah blamed Patty for corrupting Katie and putting all these ideas into her head. Patty insisted that Sarah wouldn't always be around, that

Katie needed to grow up and learn about the real world while Sarah was still there to help. Sarah just looked at Katie and told her she had twenty-four hours to get off the property and that there would be no financial support.

Katie heard Patty and Sarah arguing late into the night, but she was too busy trying to figure out what her mother meant by no financial support.

Patty came to Katie's room early the next morning. It was Katie's first lesson in finance. She knew math, but had never been taught about rent and electricity and water bills. Patty told her everything in a quick and hushed tone. She had even written out a list of all the common bills and gave Katie a lecture about debt and credit cards.

With her head spinning, Katie began to pack her belongings. How was she going to survive? She didn't have a dime and Patty said there were deposits that had to be paid before you could live somewhere. Patty had also explained about tuition. How had her tuition been paid for the past two years? She didn't know, but she bet that her mother hadn't been the one paying it.

At ten o'clock, Patty knocked on her door and came in to help Katie bring her things out to the car. The two of them drove away from the ranch and toward Katie's new future. "You are going back, right?" Katie asked, as they passed through the gate. The only time Katie had ever been past the gates was the one trip to the hospital to have her tonsils removed.

"Of course, dear. Someone has to take care of Sarah. Don't you worry. We will all be fine. Your mom will come around in time." Patty gently patted Katie's leg as she drove on.

Patty spent three days in Phoenix with Katie. They got her a driver's license, a checking account, an apartment near campus, and turned on all the utilities. When it came time for Patty to leave, Katie hugged her hard and tried not to cry. Patty gave her an envelope as she turned and left, smiling one more time and wishing Katie good luck. "You are going to be someone, Katie Freeman. Just hold your head high and learn as much as you can."

As Patty pulled away from the apartment, Katie opened the envelope. There was a check from Patty for $20,000. The simple note only said that her tuition was paid, and would always be paid. She instructed Katie to get a job, but not to work too much, as Patty didn't want her grades to suffer. She promised to send Katie what she could and asked for Katie to always keep in touch.

"Hey, Earth to Katie!" She snapped out of her thoughts as Michael gently tapped her shoulder. Everyone was looking at her. "I asked if you would like some peach cobbler," Michael said with a small smile.

"Sorry, I was lost in thought. Peach cobbler sounds amazing." Katie smiled tentatively back at Michael and worked hard to stay in the present as the conversation returned to the Underground Railroad.

Later that night, Katie wrote another letter home, this time including one for Patty.

CHAPTER TWELVE

Michael arrived to pick up Katie at seven o'clock on Monday morning. Today he was wearing a black suit with shades of orange and peach in his shirt and tie. Fighting the traffic, they arrived at headquarters shortly before eight. With Barbie safe and all leads to the abductor stalled, they had decided to spend the morning in the office catching up on their reports and looking over the autopsy findings. Katie was also interested in finding out what Lucy had discovered about David Williams.

Sitting at the computer, Michael logged on to his email and pulled up the report from Dr. Bennett. After printing two copies, he handed one to Katie, who had just dashed off an email to Lucy asking about her progress. They read the autopsy report in silence for a few minutes. "Looks like Elaine died from suffocation, though exsanguination was a close second." Katie muttered, removing her thumbnail from between her teeth. It was a bad habit she had tried to break from the time she was fourteen.

"How can she have died from suffocation?" Michael asked.

"Well, when the device is squeezed around a person, their ribs break and their spine dislocates. It causes massive pressure on the internal organs. Sometimes the ribs will puncture organs, especially the lungs. It looks like none of the ribs did that in the case of Elaine Henderson; however, as the injuries persisted, her body swelled causing further compression. She eventually was unable to breathe." Katie's recitation was said in an almost trancelike state, as if she could picture exactly what was happening. Michael regretted asking the question.

A commotion in the hallway broke her concentration as several people rushed by the door. Getting up, Michael and Katie followed the procession down the hall. They got to the elevator just as the doors were closing on Jessie and SAC Nelson. Jessie had gone into labor and had a death grip on Nelson's hand. Nelson looked as though he was going to pass out from the pain, which was amusing considering he wasn't the one in labor. As the agents all cheered and sent well wishes through the closing doors, Katie just quietly backed away and went into the break room. Not long after, all the other agents gathered to begin talking about what was happening. It appeared that the two o'clock meeting was happening early today.

Half an hour later, Katie and Michael gathered around the whiteboard in their office.

"Ok, so we have Elaine Henderson abducted on Wednesday. A search that lasted over a week with nothing, no sign of her anywhere, until she's deposited on her own front porch the following Saturday. Ten days later. This guy has to have someplace to keep the women for prolonged periods of time," Katie mused.

"Of course he does. He has an underground lair. Barbie said it had rock and dirt walls and a hard-packed floor. I wonder if he gagged them because they were near enough to be overheard, or if he just liked that they couldn't scream while he tortured them?" What had started as a smart-ass reply ended with serious questions. Michael was still unsure how far he could push Katie with his humor, but he took every opportunity to find out.

"I don't know," Katie said, "but let's not get too far ahead." Apparently she didn't get his humor, or chose to ignore it. "So he returns Elaine Saturday morning and abducts Barbara Jones on Saturday afternoon. That's a very quick turn around time for abductions. Either he had Barbie picked out before he returned Elaine, or he picked her because the opportunity presented itself. So this lair he has, it has to be secure enough that no one can escape, it has to be near enough that he can come and go without disrupting his routine, and it has to be far enough that even muffled screams aren't heard. Does that about sum it up?" Katie asked.

"Well, it also has to be easily accessible to him but difficult to find for other people. It would be hard to just build a room in your basement and bring women in and out. Neighbors would see something like that. But then, you don't want it in a random place in the woods because hunters or kids might come across it. It has to be secure, not only for the woman trapped inside, but from people accidentally finding it from outside."

Both of them stood in thought for a few minutes. Finally Katie said, "Let's move on to the torture. If he proceeds the same with all his victims, he starts by tying them to the posts in the cave and whipping them." Katie disappeared into her trance again as she talked. "So he appears behind them, uses the whip on their backside. Then moves to the front and addresses their sins. When they protest, he proceeds to whip them from the front. Judging from the shape of Elaine's body, he does this for days on end. She had evidence that the bruising had begun to heal, underneath fresh bruises."

Pausing to pick up the autopsy report, Katie studied something for a moment, once again worrying her thumbnail with her teeth. Michael didn't interrupt. He was fascinated at watching how her brain processed information. He and Stan had just batted back and forth scenarios until one seemed right. Katie disappeared into her imagination to see if she could weave the scenario that fit the evidence.

Finally, Katie resumed her story. "It says here that there was swelling around the Pear of Anguish. It appears that the muscles tore slowly. So he didn't insert the Pear and immediately open it all the way. I would assume from this that he inserted it and continued the beatings. As the days went on and she didn't confess or express remorse, he probably proceeded to open the Pear slowly, prolonging the agony."

"What makes you think that? Why couldn't the Pear be the final act? Maybe she confessed and he used that as the final punishment for whatever sin she had committed."

"Well, the autopsy says that there is evidence of irritation to the lining of her nasal passages. This would fit with the method of torture. In medieval times, they used smelling salts to reawaken a victim. The smelling salts were crystallized ammonia. I would assume that this guy is using something similar. The salts are normally harmless, but if used repeatedly or for a prolonged amount of time, they cause irritation to the mucus lining of the nose, and sometimes even to the trachea. So he would have kept waking her if she passed out. I can only imagine the pain the Pear caused. By that point in the process, she probably passed out quite often.

"Judging from Barbie's abduction, he likes his victims conscious for the torture. When Barbie passed out and couldn't be reawakened, he got rid of her. So with Elaine, he probably beat her until she passed out, brought her around and continued on. He had to release her at some point though, there isn't evidence in her joints that she hung from the posts the entire time," Katie explained.

"What evidence would show if that were the case?" Michael knew this answer; he just wanted to hear Katie's reasoning.

"Her shoulders were not dislocated, nor were her wrists. There was evidence of struggle from the ligature marks, but if she had been forced to stay upright for the entire ten days, she would have slept sometime and probably passed out for prolonged periods of time. This would mean that her entire body weight would rest on her arms, dislocating something, either her shoulder or her wrists. Based on the lack of stretching or dislocation, I'm assuming that he took her down when he was finished with the torture for the time being and strapped her down elsewhere."

Michael nodded and they lapsed back into silence. He flipped through the autopsy file once more. "There isn't any indication that she was raped or sodomized. That seems unusual."

Katie nodded. She liked that Michael threw things out there for them to puzzle through together. Her partner in Louisiana had ignored all her ideas until the case was solved. Then he liked to take credit for them. She didn't sense that with Michael. "I think you're right, that he didn't sexually assault them. Though with no fibers found on the victim and the only dirt found being common Tennessee clay, it could be that he washed them down. I don't get the feeling that he was in this for sexual gratification."

Katie looked up as if she had been struck by lightning, her eyes bugging out. "Holy cow, how could we not see this? She immediately went to the whiteboard and wrote 'CONFESSION' in front of the word 'abducted' on the timeline of each woman's disappearance. Turning back to Michael she said, "Each woman gave her confession within hours of being abducted. That has to be connected somehow."

Michael thought that through for a few minutes. "I don't see the priest as our guy here," he said. He didn't know why he thought that, just that Father Joe seemed like a gentle soul, exactly as Evelyn had described him. Not to mention that he couldn't have gotten rid of Elaine in time to get to her sister and remain visible while the search happened.

"You're right. I don't see the priest as responsible; he doesn't seem strong enough. But what about David Williams? He works at the church and could easily overhear confessions. Perhaps he sees it as his responsibility to punish the offenders. I think we need to talk to Barbara Jones and see what she confessed."

As they both reached for their jackets to head out, Lucy popped her head in the door. "You guys heading out? Got a few minutes first?"

Nodding and sitting back down, Michael and Katie looked at Lucy, waiting to see what she had to say. Lucy just dropped a file that had to be two inches thick onto the desk between them. Katie pulled it closer and looked inside. There were names and addresses listed inside. Actually, there was only one name: David Williams. Each had a different middle name or initial and a different address.

Lucy smiled as she said, "There are thousands of David Williamses out there. I need more to go on to narrow this search down. I ran the tax records for Christ the King Church, but they didn't issue a W-2 to anyone with that name. So if he is employed, it has to be on a volunteer basis. I will happily look more, but I need more information." With that, Lucy turned and headed out of the office.

Katie and Michael looked at each other, shaking their heads as they got up and headed for the door. Katie grabbed the file of people named David and took it with her.

Nearly two hours later, after fighting traffic down Interstate 24, Michael pulled into the parking lot of the hospital. Checking with the front desk, they located the room Barbie had been moved to. They found her room overflowing with family as they all tried to talk over one another. It took a few minutes for the people to notice the two newcomers in the doorway, but when they did, a hush fell over everyone. The silence was deafening.

Barbie looked up gratefully from her bed. She was exhausted and all the attention and activity was draining her further. Chuck wasn't in the room.

"Come in you two," Barbie said. Looking at her family she said, "Can you all give me a few minutes? These are the FBI agents that are looking into my abduction. I'm sure they need to ask me a few questions." Grumbling, Barbie's family made their way out of the room.

Once the room was clear, Katie closed the door behind everyone and she and Michael took seats beside the bed. "How are you feeling?" Michael asked.

Barbie groaned and Michael jumped up thinking she was in pain. Katie laughed, causing Michael to glare at her. "Oh, stop looking at me like that. She isn't in pain. She's just tired of answering that question." Turning to Barbie, the two women smiled at each other.

Barbie said, "You are so right. If one more person asks me that I might borrow your gun so I can shoot them in the knee and ask them repeatedly how they feel. I really just want to get out of this bed and walk around a little bit, but they're treating me like an invalid. Seriously, how am I supposed to get better if I'm stuck in this bed?"

"How about we help you up and we can talk while we walk the hall?" Katie asked.

The relieved look on Barbie's face said it all. Katie helped her stand up and linked their arms together, as Barbie's other hand gripped the IV pole to pull it along. With a robe wrapped around her shoulders, Barbie led the way out of the room. They walked one lap in silence before Barbie said, "Did you know I'm pregnant?" Her voice was so small it was almost non-existent.

"Yes, we heard the doctor talking to Chuck yesterday," Katie said. "I'm glad someone finally told you."

"I am having an ultrasound today to see if everything is okay. Maybe this baby will be a survivor too." The wistful tone in her voice was heartbreaking and Katie sincerely hoped that everything would be all right. Barbie didn't deserve any additional heartbreak.

Wiping her tears, Barbie turned to Katie, "I'm sure that isn't why you're here. What can I help you with?"

Glad to be back on solid ground, Katie asked, "May I ask about your confession to Father Joe the day you were abducted? I would like to know what you two talked about."

Barbie was surprised by the question. "Well, we didn't really talk about anything. I mean I have petty sins, but nothing that would be earth shattering. I told him about the little white lies I tell my mom. But really, that woman would make a saint lie. Sometimes she just doesn't get it to mind her own business. Let's see, then we talked about me and Chuck wanting to have kids. I told him about our four babies dying and how we really just wanted a baby. Other than that we didn't talk about anything else. Why?"

Ignoring her questions, Katie asked, "What do you know about David, the handyman at the church?"

"Oh, he is a sweetheart. He's very quiet. I know he was in Afghanistan and that his family used to live around here. I think they were from Kingston Springs or something. Anyway, he talks one-on-one but isn't very good around a lot of people. He says it makes him nervous to be in a crowd. He lives at the motel up by the highway. Says the owner cuts him a deal. He provides security and his room is free of charge. I think it's nice that our community still helps those less fortunate. You don't think he did this, do you? I just don't see it."

Katie smiled down at Barbie as they rounded the final corner on their third lap of the hallway. They found Chuck coming out of her room with a worried look on his face. The minute he saw her, his relief was palpable. "You had me worried, beautiful. You shouldn't be up walking." Chuck tried to pick her up, but Barbie put a hand on his chest.

"If you want to walk out of here without a gunshot wound, I suggest you back off and let me walk to my room." Chuck just smiled the biggest grin Katie had ever seen at the show of spunk from Barbie. He did back off and allow her to walk the rest of the way, though he replaced Katie as the anchor on the left side.

Katie and Michael stayed a few minutes longer, but left when the technician showed up to take Barbie for her ultrasound.

As they were leaving the hospital, Katie's stomach grumbled. Michael looked over and smiled. He drove them back to the drive thru and ordered the same meal they had the day before. Katie knew she would have to put a stop to this, but it could wait until after this meal.

CHAPTER THIRTEEN

After their late lunch, Katie and Michael returned to the church to see if David had shown up for work. They both looked forward to sizing him up. It seemed that their case hinged on this one guy. Katie didn't know why she felt this way, but David Williams was either responsible for both abductions and Elaine's murder or he knew something that could help direct their search. The sooner they talked to him, the sooner they could move forward.

When they entered the back door of the church, Katie spotted a man in the room where the search for Barbie had been coordinated. He appeared to be about six feet tall with blonde hair and blue eyes. Something about him looked familiar. He was mopping the floor in long lazy strokes. Clearing her throat to get his attention, she asked, "David?"

The man looked back at them for several long seconds before he nodded, putting the mop back in the bucket. He waved them over to a table and sat down. "You're here about Lainie."

Katie instantly perked up at the use of the nickname. "Her father called her that. How long have you known Elaine?"

"We met about a year ago. She's my little sister." David's words were spoken softly. He never made eye contact but sat still, staring at the tabletop.

Katie and Michael exchanged glances, both of them stunned. That had been the last thing they expected David to say. "I don't understand. Can you explain that to me?" Katie asked. But the admission immediately fit. He looked very similar to Elaine, and even more so like Evelyn.

"My mother left my dad when I was about five. He wasn't the nicest guy. She didn't take me along. See, mom was having an affair and the guy didn't know she was married. When mom found out she was pregnant, she knew it wasn't dad's kid, so she up and left. Guess I wasn't that important to her, either. I joined the military the minute I turned eighteen. I also couldn't wait to leave him. When I came back from Afghanistan, I found out dad had died. There wasn't anything left for me in Kingston Springs, so I looked around. I don't like people much and I have my disability pay from my service. I don't need much to live. I'm a simple guy. I like solitude and honest work. I found this position, which is volunteer and it fit my needs." David paused and looked around the room. He looked like a lost little boy sitting there.

"About seven months ago, little Austin had a school project about his family tree. Lainie helped him dig around and she came across the record of my birth to her mom. She tracked me down."

"So you two have been getting to know each other?" Michael asked quietly.

"We got together on Mondays so she could go to my therapy appointments with me. See, I have a bum leg from an old army injury. I had to have surgery about a year ago and I'm still going to therapy so I can use it properly. Hurts like hell. Then on Wednesdays we would get together for dinner before she came to church. We always met at the Waffle House by the interstate. I could walk there from my place even though she always offered to pick me up. If I had been here that night, no one would have hurt her." He finally looked directly at Katie, his eyes haunted.

"I doubt there was anything you could do. Even if you had been scheduled to work, you would have been long gone by the time she was abducted. We still don't know how he got her out of the church without being seen. What about Evelyn? How does she feel about having a brother?" Katie asked.

"I don't think Lainie had told her about me yet. Evelyn is always nice to me when she comes in the church. But she's not as outgoing as Lainie was. Guess Evelyn and I both got that from our mom." David looked up with sad eyes. He had just found a family and now it was once again taken from him.

Katie and Michael stayed a little longer talking with David, though they both knew he wasn't responsible for either abduction or Elaine's murder. He seemed so lost and lonely that neither of them wanted to leave him. Finally David indicated that he needed to get back to work, so the agents stood to leave.

As they passed into the hall, Katie continued across into the room that still held all the yard sale items. The sale was scheduled for this coming weekend. Katie began to pace the aisles, once again trying to figure out how a person could get another person out of the room without knocking anything else over. She had Michael try again to carry her out of the room, but it still was difficult to do without causing more of a mess than just the one table.

When they finally gave up and turned toward the door, both Father Joe and David stood watching them with interest. Smiling sheepishly, Michael explained what they were trying to do. Father Joe laughed. He said, "I have been wondering about that since I saw you two doing this the other night. I never would have thought of something like that. It does seem strange now that you mention it. There was not a thing out of place except the toys on the back table." He shook his head ruefully as he finished talking. "I hear you've learned about Elaine's connection with David," Father Joe said.

"Yes, he told us about his relationship with Elaine and how they met and were catching up with each other," Michael replied.

"Well, I guess I can tell you about her last confession then. Elaine was asking me about introducing her kids to David. She said Rick wasn't too happy with the relationship she had with David and he didn't want to acknowledge him. You have to understand; most people think David has PTSD or something from the war. But really he just wants the solitude and comfort of this place. Not everyone is comfortable around an introverted person, especially one who has happily taken a position associated with the downtrodden. Rick wasn't sure about David's impact on the kids. But Elaine already loved her brother. That was just her nature. She was a natural nurturer. She wanted to reach out and love everyone around her. Elaine didn't have a pretentious bone in her body. She just enjoyed helping everyone."

Michael and Katie asked a few more questions and left the church so Father Joe and David could finish their work for the night. Stepping out into the night, Katie remarked, "And just like that, we're back to square one." She sighed as she got into the car and Michael turned toward home. For the second night in a row, they made it to the B&B in time to eat dinner.

CHAPTER FOURTEEN

Michael once again picked up Katie at seven o'clock in the morning. As they drove to headquarters, they discussed what to do that day. When they arrived, Katie detoured down to see Lucy.

"Hey, just thought I would let you know I cleared David Williams from the suspect list. I appreciate all your time and effort to get me those names," Katie said. She was really trying to work on her interactions with her coworkers. She realized that the reason she never fit in with the people in Louisiana was because she never made an effort to be open with them. She just didn't know where to draw the line and always ended up erring on the side of being overcautious. She was determined to do better here in Tennessee.

Lucy looked up and smiled. "No problem. It was great to look for something besides a pervert. Well, a child pervert; I suppose when I was doing that research for you he was still a suspected pervert. Good to know he wasn't." Lucy's mile-a-minute speech never wavered. "Oh, by the way, Jessie had her baby early this morning. Little boy they named Isaiah. Eight pounds, four ounces. Tell Michael he lost the pool by one ounce...to me." She gave a gloating smile as she turned back to her computer.

"Well, thanks again," Katie said with a quick wave as she continued down the hall toward her own office.

Katie and Michael spent the morning filling out reports and throwing around theories before finally admitting that they were no closer to a suspect than they were on day one.

"What do you want to do now?" Michael asked.

Katie thought for a few seconds before saying, "Let's go see Billy Sheppard." At Michael's confused look, she explained, "You know, the guy from the cold case who wouldn't give up his source."

Michael nodded, grabbed his coat and headed out the door behind Katie.

The drive south was quicker this time, as they were running ahead of rush hour. Thirty minutes after leaving the office, they pulled up to a rundown house that at one time had been painted blue. The front porch was sagging on the right giving the house a lopsided look. The grey-haired man sitting on the left side of the front porch was shelling peas and paused in his actions as the two agents approached. Michael stepped onto the porch first and introduced himself. The man shook Michael's hand and introduced himself as Billy Sheppard. As Katie stepped around Michael to introduce herself, Billy did a double take and was so shocked he dropped the knife in his hand. Quickly recovering, he put his hand out to shake and nodded at Katie's introduction.

"Do you know my partner?" Michael asked, hoping that Katie would play along. Billy's reaction had been so strong that it set off Michael's radar.

"No, I don't think so. She just reminded me of someone from my past."

"My mom is from around these parts. You probably know some of my family," Katie said. She too had been surprised at Billy's reaction to her. Even though she didn't know where her mother was from, she thought that might be the safest way to get information from Billy's reaction.

"Nah, I'm sure it's just an old man's eyes playing tricks on me. Must be the light out here. Sun's kinda bright."

Neither of them believed Billy for a second, but chose to let the subject drop. "We're here because -"

"I know why yer here," Billy interrupted Michael, though his eyes kept wandering to Katie. It was as if he couldn't stop staring at her. "Yer old partner finally retire?" he asked.

Michael chuckled. "Yes, he did. Now you're stuck with Agent Freeman and me. Guess we'll be the ones stopping by to check on you from now on, see if you changed your mind about what happened the night Hank was shot."

"Well, now, if I remember correctly, I was having a rest in Uncle Sam's nearest facility at that time. Seems to me that I had no way of knowin' what happened to ol' Hank. Gotta tell ya, that is the luckiest night of my life. I don't mind doin' time for somethin' I done, but I sure ain't gonna take it for somethin' I ain't done."

"So you admit to selling OxyContin, but not to murder?" Katie asked.

"Honey, I admitted to sellin' them drugs years ago. I did it as a favor and don't regret it to this day. And I woulda killed that sumbitch if I'da knowed what he done. And you of all people should know to stop this insanity and let sleepin' dogs lie." With that, Billy picked up his peas and began shelling again.

"What do you mean 'me of all people'?" Katie asked, confused.

Billy just shook his head. Katie and Michael tried for another fifteen minutes to get him to talk, but he just sat in silence, shelling his peas. Finally, they gave up and left their cards on the porch railing.

As Billy watched them walk away, he thought, *"Hallelujah, Charlene made it. That girl is her spitting image."*

CHAPTER FIFTEEN

When Michael picked up Katie the next morning, she said, "Why don't we go down to Shelbyville and talk to some of the other women who were at the yard sale event the night Elaine disappeared? We should also talk to little Petey Wilson's mom, the one Barbie talked to right before her disappearance."

Michael nodded and headed south instead of north. They found Becky Wilson first at the park behind the church. Introducing themselves, they asked if she had a few minutes to spare.

"Of course. I've gone over that afternoon several times since I heard what happened to Barbie. She is so sweet; I can't imagine something so horrible happening to her. Do you know how she is?" Becky asked.

Her question was addressed to Katie, but it was Michael who answered. "She's still in the hospital, but recovering well. We walked around with her a bit yesterday."

"Oh, that is just wonderful. I know Petey thinks the world of her. She always talks to him and plays in the sandbox with him when she's here." Becky stepped away to call out to Petey about being careful while climbing the slide. Turning back to the agents she said, "What can I answer for you?"

"Can you tell us what you remember from that day? Just start from the beginning. When did you arrive? Was Barbie already here?" It was Katie who asked this time.

"Well, Petey and I got here around eleven. I thought we could play until his naptime at two. The heat helps wear him out. He's at the age where he doesn't like to nap anymore, but if he doesn't get one, he's cranky all afternoon. Saturdays my husband is generally home and we like to have a little adult time while he's sleeping." She paused in embarrassment then, her cheeks turning pink. Clearing her throat, she continued.

"Barbie showed up around 11:30. Petey saw her coming across the lawn and went running straight for her. I started to scold him for running off the playground. He isn't allowed to leave a certain area and he knows it. But when I saw it was her, I just let him go. She scooped him up and brought him right back. I heard her telling him that next time he should just wave and wait for her to get there, so he would always be safe within his boundaries. She was always teaching him something." Once again, she paused to go correct something Petey was into before coming back. "Sorry about that, a three-year-old can get into things faster than you can blink. I'm surprised he hasn't eaten all the sand from that sandbox yet." She shook her head.

Katie asked, "Do you remember anyone else here that day?"

"Well, it was so hot out Saturday that not a lot of people were here. Not to mention that T-ball and other sports are starting up. The summer leagues are beginning to play at the recreational park. I remember waving to a few people and I saw several cars come and go from the church lot, but I didn't talk to anyone else and I really couldn't say who was here. It was such a miserable afternoon. I was just hoping the heat would zap Petey's energy faster than normal. I know it was zapping mine."

Despite several follow up questions, Becky couldn't provide any further information that she thought would be helpful. Katie and Michael returned to their car to figure out where to go next.

Flipping through the file from Elaine's disappearance, they made a list of other women who had been there that night. Looking at a map of the city, they listed them in order of proximity and set off to find them.

Pulling up to Daisy Jenkins' house, they approached the front door. The house was in a newer neighborhood with cookie cutter homes. Each one blended into the next and they were so close together that they were nearly attached. Even the exterior colors blended together, providing no personality to the street.

Daisy opened the door to their knock and invited them in out of the heat. "I feel terrible about what happened to Elaine. And poor Barbie. I just don't understand. Those two never hurt anybody."

"I know it's difficult to understand how someone could do something like this." Michael began the conversation. "Can you tell me what you remember about the night Elaine disappeared?"

"Well, I know I got there a bit late. We joked that I was later than Elaine. She was never on time, bless her heart. I'm usually early, but that night, my Jimmy was running a fever and I wasn't sure I was even going to make it. My husband finally pushed me out the door. I didn't like being away when my baby was sick, so I left the church about 8:30. Things were wrapping up so I figured they would be out by nine anyway."

"What do you mean by 'things were wrapping up'?" Katie asked. Keeping her expression neutral, she felt her heart rate speed up.

"Well, we had tagged all the items except the toys. They're really the easiest part to tag. The clothes take forever, trying to sort by size and gender. It's so difficult these days to tell a boy's shirt from a girl's. Used to be you could just divide by pink and blue. Now everyone is so into gender neutral or gender inclusive. I think it's ridiculous. I have a little boy and there is no way you would catch me putting him in pink or yellow." Daisy's eyes flashed indignantly.

Katie just smiled. She fought so hard everyday to overcome opinions that men and women were different. She didn't think what color a person wore defined their gender. But she couldn't say that, so she kept her mouth shut. However, she almost burst out laughing as she caught the uncomfortable look on Michael's face as he tucked his yellow tie into his suit jacket.

Thanking Daisy for her time, they left to go to the next house.

Linda Echols lived four blocks over, but it was a vastly different world. The Echols' lived in a trailer park designed like a neighborhood. Each trailer was permanently set on a spacious lawn. The yards were all trimmed and each trailer had landscaping around the foundation blocks. There was color everywhere; even the trailers were painted in bright, festive shades. A boy of about eight answered their knock at the teal-colored trailer and told them that his mother was around back hanging laundry. Rounding the backside of the trailer, they found Linda using clothespins to hang various shirts and shorts.

Michael cleared his throat as they approached, so they wouldn't scare her. Once she looked up, they identified themselves and asked if she could answer a few questions.

"You mind if I keep hanging? In this heat they'll dry wrinkled if I leave them in the basket too long." At their affirmative nod, Linda reached down to retrieve the next item. It was a little girl's dress in various shades of tie-dyed purple and green.

"Can you tell us what you remember about the night Elaine Henderson disappeared?" Katie began.

Linda shook her head. "Such a shame, that. Poor Rick and those kids. They don't deserve this. Of course, neither did Elaine. People are saying she was tortured. I can't even think of what could happen to a person who was gone that long. I watch a lot of crime TV, so I know what goes on when someone is kidnapped. Poor Elaine. I have to stop myself every time I think of it. I just can't imagine being raped or beaten for days on end. Such a sick world we live in."

Katie and Michael exchanged looks. Obviously there were a lot of rumors floating around and they weren't all correct. "Mrs. Echols -, " Katie began.

"It's just Ms. now. And you can call me Linda. My good-for-nothing husband ran off right after Junior was born. You can bet your ass I would never have named him after that SOB if I had known he would leave me like he did."

Katie gave her a small smile and began again. "Linda, can you tell us what you remember about the gathering at the church?"

"Of course. I've been writing all this down, just to jog my memory. I was hoping I would remember something to take to Chief Davidson." Putting the final clothespin in place, she turned and waved for the agents to follow her inside.

The color explosion from outside continued inside. What she didn't have financially, she made sure to make up for in color. There were plastic and fresh flowers on every table, colorful quilts that hid the threadbare cushions of a couch dating from the 1980's, and dishes piled in the sink that were mismatched.

"Junior, I told you, you couldn't watch TV until you did the dishes." Linda grabbed the remote and shooed her son into the kitchen to do his chores. She lowered herself into the side chair, covered in yet another colorful quilt, and grabbed a notebook sitting beside her chair.

"Let's see. I got there right at seven. I don't like being late. You miss too much, see. Elaine was late as usual. We spent most of the time dividing clothes. Some of the women don't think it's right to put certain colors on kids, but I think you can never go wrong with color. It also helps keep things around longer. See, my Sally, she's a bit of a tomboy. She's forever getting grass stains on her clothes. Well, a little dye will change the color and cover the grass stain. She can wear her clothes twice as long and feel like she has a new wardrobe." Linda smiled proudly. "Some of them ladies just have too much money and not enough good sense. If they ever had to work so hard for the things they had, they might appreciate a good idea.

"Anyway, where was I? Oh, yes, the arrivals." Linda continued to ramble on and gave an account of who arrived when and what items they brought to contribute. They got a lesson on what was appropriate or inappropriate about each person. By the time Linda had refilled their tea glasses a second time, she began to wind down. "I gathered up my stuff and left about 9:15. Only Elaine and Evelyn were left. They always stay 'til everyone leaves. Elaine likes - well liked - to make sure everything was neat and tidy before she walked out the door. As far as I can tell, it was just those two and Father Joe down the hall left in the whole building. Do you think Father Joe did it? In the shows, it's always the priest." The excitement on Linda's face hadn't dimmed the entire time she talked. She was so excited to be involved in a real police investigation, and now that the FBI was involved, she was even more excited.

"We have pretty much cleared Father Joe. You can rest assured that your clergy is a good person," Michael said, trying hard not to laugh.

"Well, then that only leaves Evelyn. That poor girl. She couldn't hurt a fly. Surely you don't think it was her?"

"Now, Linda, surely you don't expect us to give away all our secrets? But tell me, if it was Evelyn, do you think she could carry her sister very far?"

Michael's tone was teasing. He was enjoying stringing Linda along.

"Oh, you!" Linda said as she giggled. "You just make sure you let me know when you find the real person. I want to know all about how you did it. Suspecting poor Evelyn! Why, that is preposterous. I can't believe you were pulling my leg." Linda fanned herself with the notebook as she chortled.

Michael bantered back and forth with Linda for a few more minutes before they got up to leave.

Once back in the car, Katie said, "I'm starving and I need a bathroom. That woman practically had us drink an entire gallon of tea. Let's find a restaurant where we can sit and talk and eat something healthier than a burger drowning in sauce." Michael smiled at Katie's grumpy demeanor, but instead of the drive thru, he took them to a local diner on Church Street, the main street running through town.

The diner was in an older building; the booths had old ripped vinyl seats and the Formica counter had chips in it. Despite the run-down condition, the place was spotless and the menu had several healthy dishes.

They waited until their food was served to start discussing all they had uncovered. Katie began the discussion. "As much as Linda delighted me with her memory, I think she had a valid point about something. What if we aren't looking for a man? We've talked several times about the fact that there is no evidence of rape. What if that's because the person doing this is female? I think it's possible for a woman to be doing this."

"She would have to be strong," Michael said. "It takes a lot of strength to subdue someone, drag them to their lair, torture them, then carry her unconscious body back to her home. If we use Linda's theory that Evelyn was the last one to see Elaine, do you really see her as strong enough to pull this off?"

Katie chewed a bite of her salad as she thought this over. "Evelyn is the last person to have seen Elaine. We only have her word that Elaine went back inside and disappeared. What if Elaine allowed Evelyn to drive her home when she couldn't find her keys? That would explain how she got out of the church with no one seeing her. So Evelyn either took Elaine to her lair, or stuffed her in the trunk until Father Joe provided an alibi. Did we ever find out what happened with Elaine's car?"

Michael pulled his phone from his pocket and dialed a number. Waiting for an answer, he waved the waitress over and ordered chocolate cake for dessert. Katie passed on her own dessert and the waitress left to put in Michael's order.

"Good afternoon, Chief," Michael said. "How are you today?" After waiting for the Chief's reply, Michael asked, "Well, Chief, I was wondering if you could tell me what happened to Elaine's car?" Michael wrapped up the call and turned back to Katie.

"Elaine's car was towed back to the Henderson house. Apparently, it was never processed for evidence. The chief didn't see the need, as Elaine didn't disappear from her vehicle. Why don't we have a team go over and look through it? Anything found might not be admissible at this point, but it might lead us to something."

Katie nodded. "I think that's a good idea. I also think we should postpone chasing down the women from the gathering that night. Today is Wednesday; so all the women will be gathered again tonight. Why not talk to them then? If anyone is missing, we can get to her tomorrow. I want to go ask Barbie a few more questions." While Michael was waving the waitress over to get the check, Katie took her fork and speared the last bite of his chocolate cake. Michael shot her a dirty look, but she just smiled back at him.

CHAPTER SIXTEEN

When Katie and Michael walked into Barbie's hospital room this time, only Chuck was there with her. Barbie had been unhooked from her IV and was gathering her belongings into a bag.

"They're sending me home," Barbie said with a huge smile as the agents walked in the door. "I can't wait to get a good night's sleep in my own bed. I mean really, how do they expect a person to recover in a place where they wake you every hour of the night and poke and prod you the entire time?" Barbie continued to stuff her meager belongings into the bag, swatting Chuck's hand every time he tried to assist.

"Congratulations," Michael said. "I'm glad you're getting out of here. Do you mind if we ask you a few more questions before you go?"

"Sure, I don't mind. It always takes them forever to get back with the discharge papers. Ask away."

Katie took over the questions. "Barbie, when the person spoke to you, how did it sound?" She was being very careful not to lead Barbie's answers.

"Hmmm, well, it was kind of raspy. Not really a whisper, but not really an actual voice. You know? Like maybe he was trying to disguise it. Do you think I know him?" Barbie was shocked at this thought. "I don't think I know anyone who could do this to a person." Shaking her head, Barbie appeared to be assessing every person she knew.

Katie gave up on trying to be vague. "What I want to know is, are you sure the person was male? Could it have been a woman disguising her voice?" Once again, Katie seemed to grasp that being direct with Barbie was better than being vague. She didn't want to cause Barbie any more worry or fear by letting her mind fill in the blanks.

Barbie and Chuck were looking at her as if she had spoken Greek, their mouth's hanging open, neither of them saying a word. Finally, Barbie began shaking her head side-to-side. "No, I'm not a hundred percent sure the voice was male," she whispered.

"Barbie, I need to ask you quite a few in-depth questions about what happened. We didn't ask you too much last time, but now that you're more stable, we really need to know a few things. Are you up to this?" Katie asked gently. Michael stood back, not entirely sure where his partners mind was or what questions - besides about the person being male - that she was going to ask. It made him nervous that she might say something to cause Barbie to have a setback.

Reaching out for Chuck's hand, Barbie lowered herself into one of the chairs in the room and nodded to Katie.

"I'm going to start with the person who took you. You said last time that he was wearing ceremonial robes. What exactly did you mean?"

"Well, you know the robes that a priest wears for special ceremonies. It was a long white robe but had a gold cape-like thing over top. It came all the way down to the floor, so I couldn't see his feet. Is it okay that I say 'he'?" Barbie asked.

Katie nodded. "You're doing really well. Can you try to think about how tall he was? Was he a lot taller than you, or close to your height? What about the hood? Could you see his eyes?" Katie stopped herself from throwing any more questions at Barbie. She didn't want to overwhelm her, but felt the need to keep her on track. It was easier to slip into using 'he' just to keep her thoughts flowing.

"I am kind of short, so nearly everyone is taller than me. I didn't really have to look up at him, so I wouldn't put him as tall as Chuck or Agent Powell. I would say definitely under six feet, maybe closer to your height, Agent Freeman."

"Can you stand up with me?" Katie asked. They both stood and Katie put herself directly in front of Barbie. Barbie raised both of her arms outward and above her head, moving her legs outward as well. She took a deep breath with her eyes closed as if she was reliving what had happened.

Katie gently said, "Just think about the guy; don't worry about what else is around you right now. You're safe now."

Barbie nodded and opened her eyes. "You're a few inches shorter than him. His head came up to my wrists when I was like this. You aren't quite that tall." Barbie lowered her arms and Chuck quickly enfolded her in his. He rocked her for a few minutes. Katie wasn't sure whom he was trying to comfort, Barbie or himself. Barbie took a deep breath and pulled back, smiling up at Chuck to reassure him that she was okay. She turned back to Katie and nodded for her to continue.

"Tell me about the hood. Could you see anything through it?

Shaking her head, Barbie said, "No, it was similar to those hoods that you see in rallies for the KKK. It was pointed on top and had eyeholes cut in it. But the light was too dim to see anything."

"Very good, Barbie. You're doing great. Let's talk about the lighting. I need you to remember the room now. Can you do that?"

"There were candles and lanterns around the room. I don't think there was electricity. Like I said before, it was like an underground cave or something. Just the pillars, I think." Barbie looked confused for a minute.

Quickly, Katie stepped in. "Tell me about the pillars. What were they made of?"

"Rock, of course," Barbie replied. "They were holding up the - *oh my goodness* - they were holding up floor joists! I was in a basement, but not a finished one. And it was really old. The joists weren't the same size as people use now to build houses. Judging by the size of them, I think the building I was under was really big. The pillars were big and square. They were the supports for the joists and there were at least six of them in a row. The room wasn't very big, maybe twenty feet long and ten feet wide." Barbie got excited as she began to remember more and more about the room.

"Barbie, how are you sure about the joist sizes and the support columns? Are you sure about the dimensions of the room?" Katie wanted to make sure that Barbie was thinking clearly. It wasn't common knowledge to be familiar with building materials.

"Of course I'm sure," she said indignantly. "Chuck works in construction and so did my daddy. I've been around buildings all my life. The materials used on that building are not used commonly today. My daddy built houses, but Chuck builds bigger buildings, like banks and churches and stuff. I've never seen joists like these used, but I know that's what they are. It had to be a big building for there to be so many supports in only twenty feet of length. I'm guessing about the width of the room. There was at least five feet in front of me, so I'm assuming the support beams ran down the middle, so there had to be at least five feet behind me too. Besides, the whip he used was about three feet long and he stood about a foot away from me. He didn't hit the wall when he swung it." Barbie shuddered at the last part as her body deflated from indignation to weariness. Chuck gently rubbed her back as she talked.

"Okay," Katie attempted to soften her approach, "so you couldn't see the whole room. Do you remember anything else in the room? Any particular smell?" Katie asked. Her heart was beating nearly out of her chest. She couldn't believe the detail that Barbie was remembering.

"There was a wooden table of some kind over to my right. It had metal on it. Not like attached to it, but laying on it. There were several curved pieces of metal on it. And there was a stairwell straight ahead of me. It was made of rock and dirt, not like a finished stairwell with wood or concrete. There were a few buckets in the corner to my right. I think I smelled cleaning solution. Maybe ammonia? I'm sorry but I really don't remember much else."

Katie smiled and grabbed Barbie's hand. "You did fantastic. Much better than I had even hoped. Are you feeling okay? Do you need us to get the doctor before we go?"

Barbie emphatically shook her head. "I'm fine. I really just want to go home." Chuck gathered her gently in his arms and held her as Katie and Michael stood to go. As they went out the door, Katie heard Chuck whisper, "Just think about our baby. Everything is going to be okay." Looking over her shoulder, Katie saw Chuck gently rubbing Barbie's abdomen. She smiled inwardly, relieved to know that nothing seemed to be wrong with the baby.

Several hours had passed as they talked with Barbie and it was nearly time to meet up with the group of ladies at Christ the King. Michael drove Katie to a nearby restaurant so they could have dinner before heading to the church. They were both silent as he drove, trying to absorb what they had learned from Barbie. Once they had settled in the same booth at the diner on Church Street and placed their orders, Katie looked at Michael and asked, "What do you think?"

Michael waited to answer as the waitress set their drinks in front of them. As the woman left the table, he answered, "Well, she wasn't one hundred percent sure her abductor was a male. That is worrisome. But I still stick with my original thought that a woman would have to be extremely strong to have pulled this off. I'm not saying it's not possible, just highly unlikely.

"I also think that the height comparison isn't very reliable. What if Barbie was standing on a platform of some kind and didn't realize it? She mentioned the floor being dirt, but did she look directly down to see what she was standing on? You're pretty tall, especially next to a woman as petite as Barbie. If the person was truly a few inches taller, that would put him at least close to six feet."

Katie rolled her eyes at the comment but chose not to make an issue out of his categorization of her. She was used to comments about her 5'9" frame. "I tend to agree with you that it's unlikely to be a female, but let's not rule it out completely just yet."

Michael nodded and they finished their meal while running over the questions they wanted to ask of the women at the gathering. Katie grabbed the bill when it arrived and paid it before Michael had a chance. "You paid for lunch. My turn," she said as she gave a cheeky smile.

Fifteen minutes later, they pulled into the parking lot of Christ the King church and circled the full lot to find a parking spot. "Do you think it's always this crowded?" Katie asked. "We need to ask that question. If the answer is yes, we need to find out where Elaine was parked that night." Michael finally pulled out of the parking lot and found a spot on the street about half a block down.

They could hear the chatter as they approached the church and stepped into the hallway. Once they entered the room and the women closest to the door spotted them, a silence spread from the front of the room to the back. Linda was sitting at a table in the center sorting girl's clothing. There were several women surrounding her and she seemed to be enjoying all the attention. She had toned down her outfit from the afternoon to include acid-washed jeans straight from 1980 and a solid sea green t-shirt.

As she spotted the agents, she stood up, shaking her hair out of her eyes. "These are the agents I was just telling you about," she announced to the silent room. A chorus of somber "hellos" responded as the group of women continued to stare at the agents. Katie, never one to enjoy being the center of attention - especially in a group of women - simply stared back. She had learned the hard way how catty women could be and had no desire to insert herself into this group's gossip.

Michael, sensing Katie's hesitance, turned on his mega-watt smile and said, "Hello, ladies. I'm Special Agent Michael Powell. Would y'all mind answering a few questions for me and my partner?" He gestured to Katie as the women began to swoon at the sight of his smile. Katie wanted to roll her eyes as several of the women started to fan themselves. She only restrained herself because she didn't want to alienate anyone; also because she had a sudden urge to find a fan of her own.

Linda walked over and slid her hand into the crook of Michael's arm and dragged him to the chair she had just vacated. Katie smiled at the look Michael sent her over his shoulder as he was led away. Choosing to remain on the sidelines, Katie waited for Michael to begin questioning the women. She had decided to watch the reactions and only speak up if she heard something interesting that Michael didn't investigate further.

Michael cleared his throat and began, "Were all of you here two weeks ago?" It was pure chaos as all the women tried to answer at once. Each was trying her best to get Michael's attention, even temporarily. At the chorus of '"yes" and "you bet" along with emphatic head nods, Michael smiled. "How about we try this a better way. Anyone *not* here two weeks ago?" Total silence descended again, everyone looked around at the women in the room, taking inventory of whom they didn't remember from the previous week.

Finally, from the back of the room came a deeper voice. "Oh, for goodness sake. I think I'm the only one who wasn't here that night." A giant of a woman stood up slowly. She was at least six feet tall with broad shoulders and short, choppy hair. She was easily 250 pounds and her arms hung down and away from her body, much like a boxer's would. The only indication that she was a woman was the size of her chest.

"Thank you," Michael said. He desperately wanted to look for Katie and see if he was dreaming this. He couldn't seem to find his flirtatious smile as the woman shifted from one foot to another. "May I ask your name?"

"I'm Claudette Lewis, but my friends just call me Dette."

Katie spoke up quickly from the doorway, "Thank you Dette, for letting us know. I'm afraid that you might be a bit bored with our questions, given you weren't here for the events of that week. I apologize now for you having to sit through this."

Michael received Katie's message loud and clear. She didn't want to tip their hand about the perpetrator possibly being a woman. Her reply was to let Michael know to move on with the other women and they would investigate Claudette later. Michael turned his head and nodded to Katie, who had her cell phone in her hand, to let her know he understood what she meant. As he turned his attention back to the women, he caught Evelyn's eyes as she lowered them to her lap. They were red-rimmed from crying and yet the tears still streamed down her face. Next to her, an elderly woman had an arm around Evelyn's shoulders, offering what comfort she could. As Michael returned to questioning the women, Katie sent a quick text to Lucy to ask her to find out all she could about a Claudette Lewis. She smiled a bit as the return text came back: *At least that's a less common name than David Williams*!

"Let's start at the beginning of the evening, shall we?" Michael began. "Did any of you arrive after Elaine Henderson?" At the multiple headshakes directed toward him, he asked, "Do you all remember where Elaine parked that night? I sure know the lot is full tonight."

"Oh, she parked in the loading zone. You know, the striped spot right beside the handicapped spots. She always parked there. We never took that spot because we all knew she would be late and would be the last one to leave. We didn't want her walking too far to her car in the dark." Linda was the one who had spoken up. All the other women just nodded in agreement.

Michael smiled at Linda. "I've already gotten a take on that night from Linda and Evelyn, why don't you all just tell me what you remember?"

Michael was about to offer encouragement for someone to start when Father Joe escorted a small woman back into the room. The woman had long blonde hair that was pulled back into a ponytail. Her eyes would normally have been a vibrant blue, but the redness and splotchy complexion gave away her anguish. One of the senior women approached and wrapped her arms around the woman. Father Joe patted her on the back as she was escorted away. He nodded to Michael, not noticing Katie, who stood immediately to the left of the door and was therefore out of his line of sight. "Agent," he acknowledged.

"I hope you don't mind us interrupting your confessions tonight, Father. We were hoping to get a better picture of what happened a few weeks ago from the other women." Michael said.

"Of course not," Father Joe replied. "Ladies, I am here if you need to talk, but for tonight why don't we take a few minutes to see if we can help Agent Powell with the investigation of what happened to poor Elaine."

At the request of a few of the women, Father Joe agreed to stay in the room. As he turned to grab a chair, he started at Katie standing behind him. "Agent Freeman," he acknowledged. He offered her the chair, but at her decline, he lowered himself down and sat back to give silent encouragement to the other women in the room.

Katie returned her eyes to the room as she gauged each woman's body language. She was curious to know about the woman who had just come in with Father Joe. The woman was distraught over something and Katie wanted to know if it had to do with Elaine, or if she was facing her own issues. Before she could ponder further, one of the women in the center of the room spoke up.

"Elaine was an angel. I don't know why anyone would do something like this to her."

"Oh, don't be an idiot," Dette said. "We all know she was having an affair." Complete bedlam broke out at this pronouncement. Michael, who was stuck in the middle of the shouting, looked desperately over his shoulder at Katie. Katie was too busy watching the action, her eyes darting back and forth trying to catch who said what. Finally Father Joe stood up and clapped his hands three times. Silence immediately descended on the group, but the anger was still present.

"I can assure everyone in this room that Elaine was *not* having an affair." Father Joe's proclamation sent a lot of "I told you so" looks toward Dette.

"Oh, come on, Father Joe. Everyone here knows she was with David twice a week and had been with him for several months. They didn't even try to hide what they were doing. Why, they were at the Waffle House in plain sight." Dette was indignant at her opinion being dismissed.

"I don't think the definition of an affair is sitting in a Waffle House," sniffed a middle-aged woman with pinched lips. Turning to Michael, she said, "I'm Gloria, by the way." She gave a simpering smile as she attempted to flirt, blinking a few extra times before she turned away.

"You wouldn't know an affair if it hopped into bed with you," Dette returned bitterly, crossing her arms over her massive bosom.

"As if you would," a third woman retorted as she stood to her feet.

"Now, ladies," Michael said with his trademark smile, "Let's not get away from the topic here. Dette, thank your for your opinion. However, we have verified that the relationship between David and Elaine was not sexual in nature."

"Oooh, can you tell us what *was* going on between them?" the third woman asked. There was a current of excitement in the room as everyone prepared to hear some unknown gossip. The whispers flying back and forth created a buzz in the room.

Father Joe stood up. "Now, ladies, don't you know what the Bible says about gossip?" Chagrinned, the women looked down. Finally, Gloria spoke up and began her recollection of events from the previous meeting.

CHAPTER SEVENTEEN

"Now, ladies, don't you know what the Bible says about gossip?" Father Joe's words nearly stopped the man's heart. Standing silent and rigid behind the secret panel at the back of the room, the man peeked through a small knot in the wood desperately trying to see who the offender was. He had already learned of another defiler this evening. *There is so much evil in this world to stamp out,* the man thought as he continued to listen and watch the conversation from the room beyond.

Michael listened as the women began to talk. As the story progressed, they each began to seek more of his attention and he heard more detail than he ever intended, from how to properly identify the gender of children's clothes to how to properly sanitize the toys. He just nodded as each woman put her stamp on the story. After finally getting to the end of the events of that night, Michael had them go over the order in which they had left. The woman who had come in with Father Joe earlier admitted to being the first to leave.

"I had to get my kids from my husband's house." Her voice hitched on the word husband.

"Do you and your husband not live together?" Michael asked gently.

"There, there, dear." The gentle old woman who had taken over comforting her upon her return to the room patted her arm gently. Looking at

Michael, she said, "Jenny is separated from her husband. And good riddance, too." Jenny broke down in tears and the woman gently led her from the room.

"Too bad her husband wasn't the one killed in that car accident," Dette said. Shocked, everyone turned to look at her. "Oh, don't look at me like that. You all know he deserved to die more than poor Lily did."

"What car accident?" Michael asked.

"Oh, about a year ago, Jenny's husband was drinking and driving... again. He ran a red light and crashed into Lily Owens's car. She died along with her three-month-old son. Terrible tragedy. Of course, it turned out she wasn't so innocent after all. She was coming home from her lover's house at the time. All while her husband was at home taking care of the other two kids." Dette was practically gleeful as she retold the story. Her entire frame vibrated with satisfaction as she told of someone else's misfortune.

"Don't you pay her no mind," Gloria said. "She likes to stir up trouble. Lily's death was tragic. And poor Jenny, she's had to move out of her own house. Her husband refused to go and she couldn't take it anymore. She moved her kids back into her momma's house, which if you ask me, ain't much better."

The man's stomach twisted with rage as he listened to the women defend each other as if their transgressions didn't exist. He would show them. Each and every one of them. He turned and went down the stairs to prepare the room for his next guest. She would join him before the night was over.

CHAPTER EIGHTEEN

Jenny turned to the little old woman who had escorted her from the room. "Thank you, Betsy, for getting me out of there," she said through her tears. "I need to get going before Jack gets too far gone and makes trouble." She leaned down and kissed the weathered cheek of the woman who was more of a mother to her than her own actual mother. Putting the strap of her purse over her shoulder, she left the church to walk to her car. She shivered as she walked through the parking lot. *Perhaps I should have had someone walk out with me, or at least watch me,* she thought. Her car was located at the far end of the lot, near the park. As she got closer, she pulled her keys from her bag and picked up her pace. She quickly unlocked the door of her 1988 Dodge Shadow. It had once been bright red, but the sun had long ago faded it to a dusty pink. She would love to have a new car, but with her minimum wage job and two kids to feed without reliable child support, she didn't see that in her future.

Quickly pulling the door closed behind her, she pushed down the manual lock and inserted the key in the ignition. Twisting the key, she heard nothing. There wasn't the click of a dead battery, or the grinding of a bad starter. There was absolute silence. Laying her head on the steering wheel, Jenny took a deep breath as she fought the tears that threatened to spill over. Without lifting her head, she turned the key once more, only to again get no response from the car.

The knock on her window made her jump and a small scream escaped before she recognized the man standing outside her car. Putting her hand to her chest, she opened the door and got out. "You scared me half to death," she said. "My car won't start."

"Why don't you pop the hood?" he replied. "Let me take a look."

As Jenny turned to reach into the car, she felt a burning sensation flow through her body as she lost control of her muscles. Before she hit the ground, the man scooped her up and walked into the woods that surrounded the park. All Jenny could think was, "Please let me get back to my kids." Darkness surrounded her as he carried her down toward Duck River.

The gathering in the church began to break up a short time later. Slowly, the women began heading toward their cars. Several of them stopped to talk in the parking lot. Michael and Katie stood on the stoop of the church and watched as, one by one, the cars began to pull out. Father Joe joined them after a few minutes of walking among his parishioners trying to calm the nerves of the women. In the end, only Betsy, Linda and Evelyn remained with the agents and Father Joe. Casually looking over the parking lot, Katie noticed four cars remained. "Father Joe, did you drive here tonight?" she asked.

"No, I live in the parsonage, just through those trees." He gestured to the left of the lot away from the direction of the river. "I don't ever drive over. In fact, I rarely drive at all. Usually only to the grocery store and back. Why?"

Katie ignored the question and turned to the women. "Which cars in this lot are yours?" Each of them turned to point out their cars. Michael had taken a look around and knew immediately what the problem was. Once the women's three vehicles had been identified, Katie asked, "Then whose car is that?" as she pointed to the back of the lot.

"Oh, no!" Betsy said. "That's Jenny's car." She turned terrified eyes to Father Joe. "Please tell me he didn't get her, too."

Michael and Katie took off running toward the car, but Katie knew what she would find. Jenny had been the first to leave and she had left significantly earlier than anyone else. Reaching the car, Michael shined the small flashlight on his key ring into the car. Sitting on the passenger seat was Jenny's purse and hanging from the ignition were her keys. Michael looked up into four pairs of anguished eyes as the three women and Father Joe made it to the car. He just shook his head as Betsy burst out crying.

"I should have walked her out. Oh, why did I let her leave alone?" Her heartbroken cries were the only sound as Michael pulled his phone from his pocket to call Chief Davidson.

Father Joe gently led the women back to the church. Katie pulled gloves from her purse and put them on as she began to search the ground around the car for evidence.

Chief Davidson arrived fifteen minutes later followed by what seemed to be every squad car in the county. The flashing lights from the tops of the car were enough to light an entire city block. One thing was for sure: if there were any other crimes in the city that night, the criminal didn't have to worry about getting caught.

"Son of a Buick!" Chief Davidson exclaimed. "How is it that you were right here and that SOB managed to kidnap another woman? Were you just sitting here with your thumb up your butt? Or did you just decide to bring your blindfold tonight? I mean, Son of a... Son of a...," Chief Davidson couldn't seem to think of another noun to keep from cursing. Finally he spat out, "Son of a Biscuit Eater!" With that, he left a gaping Father Joe and Agent Powell in his wake as he spun on his heel and began barking orders to his deputies.

As Chief Davidson's men began to organize for a search, Katie held up her arms to signal for quiet. "I found a few muddy boot prints around Jenny's car. They are faint. Before you all go traipsing around the parking lot and the woods, would you allow me to see if I can track them? Chief, could you have your crime scene people come photograph these and see if any are clear enough for a cast?" Picking up a flashlight from the supplies the deputies had been laying out, Katie began walking the parking lot following the prints. Michael kept everyone back so they didn't destroy any evidence. They didn't know if the prints were from the kidnapper or if Katie had found anything further; he just didn't want to have the deputies compromise any more of the scene. Once Katie reached the end of the lot, she turned and said, "There's a clear print here. Let's get this cast and photographed. I need two or three people to come with me to see how far we can follow the tracks."

"I'm Deputy Tom Fuller, ma'am. I'm the best tracker in the county." Tom was all knees and elbows. He looked like a middle school kid and his face was still full of acne. At the nods from those surrounding him, Katie decided to take him at his word.

"Great, then let's move. This guy already has a good head start on us. Anyone else you think we should bring?"

Tom waved over his partner, a hulking man who looked like he could bench press a car. He introduced him as Jerry Spires, and the trio headed into the woods. Katie didn't understand why Michael chuckled at the introduction. She thought it was a bit rude to be laughing at the poor man, although she didn't know which one he was laughing at. But she didn't have time to question him about it, especially since he stayed behind to organize the search once Katie let them know what they found.

When Michael turned around, he discovered that nearly every car that had recently left the church had returned; most with additional occupants. The women had brought their husbands, sons, fathers, and anyone else they could gather to aid in the search. "Chief, do you see Jenny's family? Is there anyone you can spare to go round up the estranged husband? It would be interesting to know if he's home and how he reacts to the news."

Chief Davidson nodded and called two deputies over. After giving them the task of going to get Jack Downing and the kids and then notifying Jenny's mother, Geraldine Simon, the Chief turned back to the sign-up lists of the searchers.

Michael kept an eye on the woods where Katie and the two deputies had disappeared as he listened to the Chief divide the searchers. They were gathering in their groups waiting for the signal to begin searching. Ten minutes turned into twenty and then to thirty. Michael was about to give the call to send the searchers out, if only to see if they could find Katie when he saw the shine of three flashlights returning to the lot. Breathing a sigh of relief that he told himself was because he didn't want to break in another new partner, Michael went to meet the three as they emerged.

"We lost the tracks in the river. We thought it would be better to head back and get help to search the banks and see if we can find where the tracks emerge from the water." Katie continued across the parking lot as she spoke. As the four of them reached Chief Davidson's side, Katie said, "All right everyone, Deputy Fuller is going to give directions to where we need to start the search. It's important that you move quickly, but remember to be thorough and careful of your footing. Because of the time of night and the darkness, we would like all search parties to return by midnight. If we don't find anything by then, we will resume tomorrow morning. Deputy." Katie nodded to Tom to take over.

Tom gathered the leaders of each of the search groups and brought them over to the city map spread out on a picnic table. Katie leaned over to Michael and asked, "Why were you laughing at Deputy Fuller? It isn't polite to laugh, especially when we need to keep up our relationship with them." Katie hadn't forgotten the incident from before she left.

It took Michael a minute to realize what Katie was talking about, but as it dawned on him, he smoothed out his furrowed brow and smiled. "Oh, come on. Tom and Jerry?" At Katie's confused expression, Michael was astounded. "Surely you have heard of Tom and Jerry? You know the cat that chases the mouse in the cartoons?" As Katie continued to look at him blankly, he just shook his head. "I see I'm going to have to catch you up on some of the finer television shows of the past few generations." He smiled as he said it, but Katie was once again aware that she was different, even when all she wanted to do was blend in.

Shouting from the lot caught their attention just then. Two deputies were wrestling a man out of the back seat of a police cruiser. Obviously intoxicated, the man struggled and screamed against the manhandling from the officers. "Get your filthy pig hands off of me you bastard! I told you I don't care what happens to that bitch. She can't even bother to come get her brats on time. Why don't you just take them to her mother's house and leave me in peace?" The man jerked his whole body back attempting to break the hold. Unfortunately, the deputies had just gotten a signal from the chief to release the man and his resistance caused him to fly backward. Tripping over his own feet, the man landed on his butt right next to the car door he had just exited. The two little boys who were about to climb out of the car behind their father quickly shrank back into the interior of the vehicle. Jack Downing just laid his head back against the fender and with one final belch, passed out.

Geraldine Simons quickly stepped forward and shepherded her grandchildren out of the police car and into her own. "I'm taking them home and getting them fed. If you do find Jenny, make sure she knows I've got 'em." With that she drove away from the search area. Katie caught Betsy shaking her head as the woman left. "If that was my daughter out there, I wouldn't rest until I had ripped up every tree in that forest," Betsy said as she resumed pouring coffee for the searchers.

Everyone turned away from the unconscious form of Jack Downing and carried on with the business at hand.

The search continued until midnight, when all the parties had returned empty handed. Michael and Katie sent everyone home with a request for volunteers to return at eight in the morning to begin again.

The man got in his car along with all the other searchers and headed toward his home. He had barely had time to get an unconscious Jenny undressed and tied to the pillars before he returned to see if anyone noticed her missing. He'd made it back to the parking lot just as the two agents discovered her car left in the lot. He had quickly and quietly slipped through the trees and out onto the street where he'd parked his car. Sitting in the drivers seat, he waited until several other townspeople began making their way back to the church. Calmly, he pulled in behind them and stayed close enough to keep an eye on what was happening.

He nearly had a heart attack when he learned that he had left footprints in the dirt. As an avid woodsman, he had no trouble being chosen as the leader for one of the search teams. As he led the group along the bank of the river, over the exact trail he had taken nearly two hours earlier, he kept a close eye for any signs that he had been through the area previously. He caught sight of one of his boot prints and surreptitiously wiped it away. He was also careful not to leave any additional prints while walking with the search party. He knew he would have to ditch his work boots once he got out of there.

His group made it all the way to the camouflaged entrance to his hideaway, right in the bend of the river, before they had to turn back. He made a show of glancing around and made sure to ask the others to do so as well. He wasn't worried that they would find his tunnel, he had done a masterful job of disguising it. His father had taught him how to weave branches and leaves together to make a deer blind while hunting and no one in the county did a better job of it than the men in his family.

When no one had seen anything of interest, he turned them around and headed back to the church. They had arrived back just in time to see Jack Downing make his entrance. He tried his best not to be overly antsy as the rest of the searchers returned, but he really wanted to get out of there. Didn't these people understand that he needed to show Jenny the error of her ways? Didn't they understand that the only way she would come back was if she confessed and truly repented? She must survive her punishment before he would forgive her sins, for only through his righteousness and mercy could the truly repentant be set free.

He parked his car in the driveway and made his way inside, turning on lights as he went. Making his way to the master bedroom, he quickly changed shoes and took his old boots along with him as he exited the back door of his house. Entering the woods from the opposite side from the church, he dropped the boots into the river and watched the slow current carry them down. He thought he would have to wade out into the river as the shoes caught on a rock, but they eventually worked free and continued their journey downstream.

A few minutes later, he entered the tunnel and silently made his way toward the room at the end. Jenny was awake and looking around, struggling to free her arms. He could smell her panic in the sweat that glistened down her back. Removing his own clothing, he slipped the robe over his head and put on the hood. He had borrowed the hood and robe from his grandfather's closet. The old bastard was dead now and there was no one left to care that the robe and hood from the formerly highest-ranking KKK member in the state were missing. He had also borrowed the Humeral veil from the former priest of Christ the King. The ceremonial cape was the same one Father Nicholas always used when giving the sacraments. It was important that he have this wrap because he wanted the offenders to know he was offering to cleanse them.

Picking up the whip from the ground beside the hooks that now held his clothes, he approached Jenny. He felt his anger toward Jenny grow as his body reacted to her nudity and fear. She was another man's wife and yet she still tempted him. He would have to teach her the proper respect for the sanctity of marriage. A woman shouldn't tempt another man. Raising his arm, he began to rain down blows on her backside. As she cried out and struggled against her bonds, his body heated with excitement making him angrier. Her cries were little mewls that made him ache to penetrate her. But he wouldn't; no he couldn't. She belonged with someone else and he would show her that her vows were sacred and ensure she never violated them again.

Lowering his arm, he walked around to face her. Her body sagged with relief that the blows had stopped. Her breathing came in short choppy breaths as she struggled to breathe around the iron in her mouth; her nose congested from the tears. As her arms began to ache from the weight of her body, she shifted, trying to find a way to curl into herself.

"You have committed adultery. You have lain with a man who is not your husband," he whispered.

She began shaking her head, begging him to understand that he was wrong. Her defiance heightened his anger and once again he raised his arms and let the whip connect with her skin. The whistle of the whip through the air ended in a sharp stinging slap against her breasts, stomach and thighs as she again struggled to avoid the impact. But her bonds held tightly.

Finally, winded, he lowered the whip and moved behind her again. Removing the lid from the basin, he brought a cloth saturated with water and frankincense and began washing her back. The oil both burned and soothed the cuts. As he washed her, he chanted:

> *Have mercy on her, O God,*
> *because of your unfailing love.*
> *Because of your great compassion,*
> *blot out the stain of her sin.*
> *Wash her clean from her guilt.*
> *Purify her from her sin.*
> *For I recognize her rebellion;*
> *It haunts me day and night.*
> *Against you, she has sinned.*
> *She has done what is evil in your sight.*
> *You will be proved right in what you say,*
> *Your judgment against her is just.*
> *Purify her from her sins,*
> *She will be clean.*
> *Though she will be crushed and broken,*
> *She will be happy once again.*

Jenny recognized the verses from Psalms, though several parts were missing or altered. The closing lines filled her with terror. All she could do was pray that *her* God truly did intervene.

Once the man had finished cleansing her body, he untied her, keeping a firm grip on her hands. He led her to a wooden table, placed her on it and tied her arms and legs to each corner. "We will try again in the morning," he said and walked away.

He quickly changed back into his clothing and made his way down the tunnel and back to his house. He knew he wouldn't sleep well, knowing she was waiting for him. He would break her pride and she would admit her transgressions. Turning off the lights, he lay down in his bed and finally took pleasure in reliving Jenny's silenced screams.

CHAPTER NINETEEN

Katie didn't sleep at all that night. She and Michael had returned to the B&B around one thirty, but try as she might, she couldn't stop her brain from reliving Barbie's tale but substituting Jenny's face. Barbie had only suffered a small fraction of what Elaine Henderson had and Katie had been around enough evil in the past three years that her mind could fill in the blanks between where Barbie's torture ended and the condition of Elaine's body when it ended up on her own front porch. Every time Katie started to drift off, she imagined she heard Jenny's muffled screams. Katie could only hope that the person doing this prolonged the whipping, that he didn't begin using the other implements too soon. She just had to hope that they found Jenny before he escalated the process.

Katie gave up the pretense of sleeping at five and wandered down to the kitchen. She made herself a cup of chamomile tea and was stirring honey into the cup when Michael walked into the kitchen. Michael had stayed in the guest room instead of driving the extra distance to his house. He still kept clothing in his old room in the house from before he had moved out. Michael froze as he entered the room. He had never seen Katie with her hair down and didn't realize the glossy, dark masses extended all the way to her waist. He fought the urge to move forward and feel if them to see if they were as soft as they looked.

Shaking off the thought, Michael took a deep breath and stepped through the doorway. "Got an extra cup?"

Katie jumped and nearly scalded herself as the tea splashed over the rim of her cup. "Sure. Guess you couldn't sleep either, huh?" Katie poured a cup of tea and handed it to Michael. As he turned to add sugar, she quickly scooped her hair up and pulled it into a sloppy bun that she tied with the band on her wrist. She could hear her mother's voice in her head. *A woman's hair is her crowing glory. Don't ever show it lightly and never to someone who doesn't deserve you.* Katie had been gone from home long enough to know that her mother's point of view wasn't exactly normal, but all the years of conditioning were difficult to overcome.

When Michael turned back around, she could see the disappointment in his eyes. Choosing not to acknowledge it, she said, "I couldn't stop hearing Jenny's screams and seeing what he was doing. We desperately need a break in this case." Katie began chewing on her thumb as she thought through what they knew so far.

"Well, I suppose we can rule out Claudette," Michael said. "She was still in the church with us when Jenny disappeared. I suppose we can also rule out Jenny's husband. He was pretty far gone last night when he was picked up. I think we should still talk to the kids just to make sure he didn't leave the house last night. But I don't think he could have gotten that intoxicated between when Jenny disappeared and when he was brought to the scene."

"You're right," Katie agreed. "We don't seem to be getting anywhere with this case. At least this time we know how he got to her. I keep going back to Elaine Henderson. I think whoever took her waited for Evelyn and Father Joe to come back inside. While they were in the back of the church, he had to have snuck out the side door. That is the only door where no one would see him. Of course that still doesn't tell us where he took her. Maybe tomorrow we should examine the flowerbeds around that door and see if there are any footprints. The rain we had the other night probably obliterated anything that remained, but maybe we'll get lucky. That seems to be the only way we're going to get anywhere with this case."

Caroline walked in right then. "I thought I heard people up and about. Can I make you all breakfast? You'll be heading out soon."

"Please, don't go through any bother on our behalf." Katie hated that they had woken anyone up. She wasn't used to having anyone in the same house, so her nighttime review sessions didn't normally disturb anyone. Katie could easily go with only a few hours sleep, though the coming day would be challenging with no sleep at all.

Katie and Michael arrived back in Shelbyville at 7:30. Father Joe and David were already there, making coffee and setting up a table of donuts for all the volunteers who would be arriving. Within fifteen minutes, two more tables had been set up to hold all the food the elderly women from the community had brought. Betsy showed up bearing three dozen buttermilk biscuits and at least two gallons of homemade sausage gravy. Several other women had brought additional biscuits, trays of scrambled eggs, toast, English muffins, jelly, bacon and sausage patties. By 8:00, nearly a hundred people had arrived and were being organized into search parties. Tom Fuller was once again in charge of the search coordinates and assigning people to various terrain. The temperature had already soared to the low eighties, which promised that this day would be miserably hot and very humid, more like late June instead of mid-May.

Michael decided to go out with the search parties this morning, which left Katie to stay behind at the church to help with coordination and also to follow up on a few ideas she had. Not wanting to be rude, Katie took an English muffin and added strawberry jelly then made her way to the table which held the sign-up lists of volunteers. Pulling out her laptop, Katie began cross-referencing the names of the volunteers with the women who had been at the gathering the night before. Betsy came to join her a few minutes later. "Can you help me put names to faces?" Katie asked her.

"Sure, honey, let me see." Betsy lifted her reading glasses, which were hanging from a chain around her neck, onto her face. "Well, I am sure you remember Claudette, she stormed out last night while I was talking with Jenny in the hallway. That woman just needs some prayer, such bitterness." Betsy shook her head as she thought of Claudette. Taking up the names again, Betsy listed the women and where they had been sitting the evening before. She commented on when they had left, if she remembered seeing them head out. Finally, she was down to herself, Elaine and Linda. "I think every woman from the meeting has returned either last night or this morning, some of them both times. I don't know what you hope to find, but I don't think it's any of them." Betsy sent a look toward Katie to let her know exactly how unlikely Betsy thought it was that the person they were looking for was in that group.

"Thank you, Betsy. I'm just trying to get a feel for everyone here and how they relate. I think being an outsider here isn't making this any easier." As Katie finished speaking, two shadows fell across the table. Looking up, she saw Lucy and Andy standing before her with two cases of electronic equipment.

"Man, it's so hot I just saw two trees fighting over a dog," Andy said as Katie looked up. At her confused expression, Lucy laughed.

"Girl, you're going to have to learn some southern expressions if you expect to stay around here. Another of his favorites is 'It's hotter than two squirrels making love in a wool sock,' but don't let him catch you laughing, it just encourages him." Lucy said all this as she pretended Andy wasn't there and she began pulling her computer equipment from the bag slung over her arm. "We've escaped the loony bin to pay you a visit, see if we can help out down here. This doesn't seem to be going your way. Where's Michael?" As usual, Lucy talked a mile a minute, her hands moving as fast as her mouth. Lucy plopped down in the chair Betsy had vacated and began turning on the power to her laptop. Andy pulled a chair up on the other side of Katie.

"Don't you listen to her," he said. "I happen to know all you need to survive the south. And all that knowledge is yours for the small price of a date with yours truly." Andy wiggled his eyebrows suggestively as he leered at Katie.

"Now young man, don't you be getting fresh with the ladies," Betsy said as she put two plates heaping with food in front Andy and Lucy. "You show them the proper respect." With that she turned and walked off. Katie and Lucy struggled to contain their laughter at the shocked expression on Andy's face.

"At least she let me keep the food," Andy said as he began shoveling food into his mouth, half afraid that Betsy would come back and take it away.

Once Lucy and Andy had finished their food, Lucy got down to business. "I did a search on Claudette Lewis. Interesting family. Father Claude Lewis, mother Yvette Lewis. They had four children, three daughters: Claudette, Claudanne, and Claudine; one son, Claude Jr. Kind of reminded me of George Forman, but at least there was some variation. Family owns and operates a horse farm on the edge of town. All four children live at home, only Claude Jr, is married. Now, Claudette is a piece of work. She was on her high school wrestling team and was training at one time to be an Olympic weightlifter. She had an accident involving one of the horses and those dreams were shattered. Apparently she's been a little bitter since then. She was arrested a few years ago for public intoxication and fighting. She started a brawl in one of the bars here in town. A little community service and all was forgiven. There isn't so much as a speeding ticket on her record for the past three years." Lucy stopped to take a breath and Andy picked up.

"Now, otherwise down at 'All Claude's Children' ranch -" Andy paused and took a little bow at the shocked expressions from Lucy and Katie. "Okay, I made that name up, but it works, right?" The women just shook their heads and groaned, trying not to encourage him. "Anyway, the other mini-Claudes aren't much better. The whole family is known for their tempers and their drinking. Police are involved in nearly every trip the Lewises make to town. Apparently a trip to the grocery store is cause for a good family fight. But I have to say, I don't see any of them for this spree. None of the offenses are in line with what we see from this guy. The Lewises are pretty happy to keep their conflict in-house. With the one exception in the bar with Claudette, nothing else appears to involve others."

Katie chewed her thumbnail as she thought over the findings on Claudette Lewis. "I think you're right. Michael and I thought she was still in the church when Jenny left so we had pretty much ruled her out. But Betsy thought she left about the same time as Jenny, so I was curious about what you found. Let's not completely eliminate her, but we can move her down to the bottom of the list. What can you pull on Jack Downing? He's the husband of the current missing woman, Jenny Downing. From what I gather, they're separated and he isn't the friendliest of guys. When he was brought here last night, he was already at the point of passing out drunk. I'm not sure I see him for it, but we have to look at him as the spouse of a missing person."

As Katie talked, Lucy's hands flew over the keyboard. "Well, well, what have we got here?" Lucy said. Her shirt was stuck to her back and sweat poured down her face. "Other than the pending vehicular manslaughter charges from a drunk driving accident a year ago, there isn't too much. Seems Jack likes to get rough. There are several reports of domestic violence, a lot of drunk driving arrests, and several drunk and disorderly charges. Seems he didn't just start with Jenny, either. Jack is about ten years older than Jenny and was married twice before her. Both previous wives pressed charges against him and have restraining orders in place. They both have custody of the children he fathered. Seems Jack pays most of his check in child support to the other two women. Six children with three different women; first wife has one child, second wife has three and then two with Jenny. It would make sense that he wouldn't want a third divorce. Hell, he couldn't afford to live and pay support for that many kids. His life would be easier if his wife just disappeared."

"Well," Katie said, "I don't know if that's the case. I didn't get the feeling that he liked his kids much. Can you see if he actually pays the support, or if it's just in the divorce agreement?"

"I can answer that." The three agents looked up at a blond-haired woman. Katie had to look twice; she looked so much like Jenny that they could have been twins. "I'm Tiffany, Jack's first wife. And yes, we all look alike. He has a type. Jack doesn't pay me or Melissa a dime, but we don't complain. See, if we pushed him for the money, he would insist on visitation. The kids are afraid of him and he really doesn't like them. He would only force the visitation if we forced the money issue. So instead, we just let it go. When I heard Jenny was missing, I had to come see if it was Jack's doing. Do you think she was taken by the same guy who got Elaine and Barbie?"

Andy and Lucy both bent their heads over the computer leaving Katie to answer the questions and deal with Tiffany. "Do you know Elaine and Barbie?" Katie didn't want to give too much away, but she thought Tiffany could provide helpful insight into Jack Downing's personality.

"Of course, this is a small town. I go to church here, but my work schedule doesn't allow me to join the Wednesday night group. My son is in the same school as Elaine's children. We see each other at sporting events mostly, especially soccer. Barbie and I went to school together, along with Jack, though he was a few years older. Barbie helps out with my son on nights when I need a babysitter. She's really great with kids. Such a shame what happened to both of them."

"Tiffany, I'm going to ask a very personal question. I hope you'll answer, but if this is too difficult, I can get an answer another way." At Tiffany's nod, Katie asked, "Can you give me details about when Jack assaulted you? What set him off? Were the assaults usually the same? What did they entail?"

Taking a deep breath, Tiffany began divulging what life was like with Jack. "Well, it didn't take much to set him off. Dinner wasn't good, we were out of beer, I was late getting home - you name it and it set Jack off. He liked to hit with an open hand. He said he liked the sound of it and how it made my skin turn red. He also said it took longer, whereas when he punched, the punishment ended too soon. It always ended with us naked and him forcing himself on me. Do you need details about that?" Tiffany was looking at her hands in embarrassment.

"No, I don't need those details. Thank you for answering." Katie reached over and laid a hand on Tiffany's knee. "I think that's all I need to know for now. Thank you again for coming and talking to me."

"I know Jack is bad news, but if this is the same person who took Elaine and Barbie, I just don't see Jack doing it. There are rumors that Elaine was pretty messed up when she was found. That isn't Jack's style. He likes the thrill of a woman submitting to him, but he wouldn't tie her up, that would take the fun out of it for him." With that, Tiffany walked over to the food table to help set out lunch and serve it to the returning searchers.

Michael and his search team returned to the church at two that afternoon. They were tired, sweaty and hungry, but had found no sign of Jenny Downing. Michael grabbed a bottle of water from the table and downed it in one long drink. Tossing it in the trash, he grabbed another bottle and then made his way through the food line. Once he had loaded a plate with a pulled pork barbecue sandwich, potato salad, pasta salad, and several vegetables, he sat down between Lucy and Katie to catch up on what he had missed.

Katie ran through all the research they had done on the various people of interest and also the interviews she had conducted, ending with, "Every time something looks promising, we end up right back where we started. The only good thing I can see right now is that I don't think Jenny is in danger until the end of the day today." When her comment was met with blank stares and confused looks from the other three agents, she explained, "I think this guy is a productive member of society. I think he holds a regular nine-to-five job. If he didn't, people here would be pointing fingers. That means that whomever he is, he is at work right now, so Jenny is somewhere secure in his lair."

"That's an interesting theory," a deep voice said from behind Katie. "Care to enlighten us as to how you came to be of that opinion?" Turning, Katie came face-to-face with SAC Nelson and ASAC Perry.

Never blinking, Katie explained, "Well, we have suspects with questionable pasts. However, even their previous assault victims come to their defense. These people have jobs, families, lives; for all intents and purposes, their past behavior should have the people of this town throwing them under the bus. Instead, as long as these people are interacting with the community, they are considered innocent. The only person they were willing to offer up was David Williams, and he really was innocent. But because he keeps to himself, everyone was suspicious. So, this guy has to be involved in the town somehow. From my experience, I think this is someone who likely grew up here. Someone everybody knows and they probably know his family. I think he will work a blue-collar job, something in skilled labor. I don't think he holds an office job, or is educated past high school. But again, that is just a guess based on past experience."

Nelson and Perry had pulled chairs up to the table. As Katie finished speaking, they both just looked at her, offering neither support nor criticism. Katie just returned their looks, refusing to back down from her position. Finally, Nelson nodded. "We've had a request for you to return to Louisiana. It appears they have a serial killer in Baton Rouge. Doesn't look like your former partner can keep the same closure rate, now that you're not there."

Katie worked hard not to squirm in her seat or to let the smile she was holding back show. Her former partner was a prick who loved nothing better than talking up *his* success. Because Katie was quiet and didn't challenge him, everyone assumed she was riding his coattails. It had never mattered to Katie who received credit, as long as the bad guy was off the street. Knowing now that her former office had requested her transfer, it made her want to dance that they were seeing what they had tossed away. Only the thought that there was a serial killer on the loose sobered her mood.

"It seems you're in the middle of an important case here, though. I don't know that we can spare you," Nelson continued.

"You're damn right, we can't spare her," Michael chimed in. "She's going to solve this case here soon. Her mind sees things that mine doesn't. I mean," Michael paused, trying to organize his thought to get his point across correctly, "our investigative styles oppose each other and we are resolving issues much faster than I used to with Stan." Michael's face turned red as he bumbled through his explanation. He was glad to be working with Katie, their styles just meshed. Their strong and weak points complemented each other. But voicing that out loud was awkward.

"Hmm…" was all Nelson said as he rose from his chair. "Well, we hadn't seen you two in the office in days. Thought we'd come out to where the action was and see if you needed anything more than Boggs and Dillon." He nodded to Lucy and Andy as Perry followed him to his feet. "I look forward to reading your reports and seeing you back in the office at some point. Bring that lady home." With that, he and Perry returned to their car and drove off.

The next round of searchers headed out at four. This time Katie and Lucy joined two separate parties. They searched until sundown before returning but none of the parties had anything to report. Sending everyone home with a request for volunteers to start over at first light, Katie and Michael made their way back to Smyrna.

CHAPTER TWENTY

Dinner was a quiet affair at the B&B. Katie and Michael were absorbed in thoughts of the case. The kids tried several times to draw them into conversation, but finally they just turned to their parents and each other to talk. Caroline jolted Katie out of her thoughts when she said, "Oh, Katie, you received a letter today."

Katie's head snapped up. "I did?" she said with confusion. Katie hadn't received a letter from anyone since she'd left Phoenix. To be fair, she hadn't provided an address to anyone back home since she graduated from the FBI Academy, either. She knew that Patty would have continued writing to her. But Katie didn't want to add to her stress, and the words Patty used in her letters showed that there was enough strain already. So she continued writing without providing a means for them to write back. When Katie had sent the letter last week, she had included a return address on the envelope. She didn't know why, just that something about this place seemed like home, so adding the address had just felt right.

Caroline got up and went to the office at the back of the house. She returned a few minutes later with an envelope in her hand. Katie looked down to see Patty's familiar handwriting. At first she felt happy, knowing that Patty still cared enough to write. Then a feeling of sadness came over her as she realized her mother had still not forgiven her. She wondered if her mother even loved her anymore. She had never doubted it growing up. Her mother had always played with her and they had spent endless hours laughing as they explored the ranch and planted or harvested the garden. Her favorite memories were of standing in the kitchen, first watching - and as she grew up - helping to can the vegetables.

But as Katie had reached adolescence and began asking questions that her mother didn't want to answer, the distance between them grew. Katie had never understood why her mother didn't want her to know certain things. She also never understood why her mother never left the ranch. When Katie turned sixteen, she dreamed of walking through those gates and never coming back. Katie saw those gates as her prison. It wasn't until she was in a psychology class her first year at Arizona State that she realized her mother saw the gates as her security. Katie just wished she knew what her mother feared outside those gates.

Reaching up, Katie took the envelope from Caroline, excused herself and left the room.

"Who was that from?" Michael asked.

"I don't know, but the return address was in Phoenix."

Michael just nodded as he looked to the stairway. He knew Katie was from Phoenix, but she hadn't seemed happy to have a letter from home. And who sent letters through the mail nowadays? He always emailed or texted his parents, even though they were in the same city. He would just have to find a way to get those answers. Katie was behind on telling him a daily fact about herself, anyway.

Walking up to her room, Katie closed the door behind her and made her way over to the window seat. She stared at the envelope for a good five minutes before turning her attention to look out the window. She was afraid to open the letter, but excited at the same time. She wanted desperately to know what was going on back home, but was scared that Patty would finally tell her to stop writing. Twenty minutes of internal arguments later, Katie picked up the letter and opened it.

My dearest Katie,

I am so glad to finally hear from you after all this time. You haven't written home in months. Your mother and I were beginning to worry about you. I could see it in your mother's face every time I returned from the mailbox. While she won't admit so out loud, she misses you terribly and is so proud of all you have accomplished.

We have a house full of residents at the moment. Domestic violence never ends. I suppose I don't need to tell you that, what with your line of work. Your mother has finally allowed women with sons to come onto the property, but only if the boys are younger than ten. I think that is progress. After all these years she still won't open up and tell me what happened to her. I can only imagine that it must have been too horrible to ever speak of. Though I do think counseling would help her, I can never get her to leave the ranch to go.

Enough of that nonsense. The willow tree outside your old bedroom window blew down over this past winter. It makes me sad every time I go in to dust your room. I remember the hours you used to sit at that window and daydream of better places. More importantly, I remember catching you climbing out your window to sit in the branches of that tree. You always said you could dream bigger in the great outdoors. Your room is still exactly as you left it when you left home. Here I am getting misty eyed over you and you've been gone for eight years.

We could really use your room for the guests we have right now, but your mother won't hear of it. I keep telling her she's wasting her time hoping you will come back. That the only way you will ever do that is if she writes to you and invites you. Seems your mother is very stubborn and prideful. But I suppose you already know that, seeing as you are so much like her.

I don't want to worry you, but I do think you should know that your mother isn't looking well lately. She is tired a lot and has lost weight that she really can't afford to lose. I have the doctor coming next week to check up on her. I do think that she should go to the hospital and have more tests run than can be done here. She won't hear of it. She says she bought this land to live her life in peace and she won't leave it ever again. She wants me to petition the county to allow her to be buried here. She says she doesn't even want to leave in death. I just don't understand her sometimes. Now, don't you worry about all this. I will write to you as soon as we see the doctor. I probably shouldn't have mentioned anything in this letter anyway. It's just that you haven't given me a place to write back to in so long.

Well, now I should confess. I have looked you up on the internet when I'm in town at the library. I just *needed to know where you were. It's so much easier to keep track of the headlines when I know what city to look in. I was so proud when I read the headlines about your cases in Louisiana. You seemed to be doing so well. I have to say I didn't like that partner of yours. He seemed arrogant. Why you never spoke up about your cases is beyond me. He hogged all the spotlight. However you ended up in Tennessee, I'm glad you're not with that guy anymore.*

Tell me more about your new partner. Is he better than the prick? I keep hoping one day you will meet a hunk and fall in love. Perhaps your new partner... Oh, you know how I am. I always read romance into everything. HA! But I suppose it never hurts to escape reality. I just hope your new partner isn't an old, portly man. That really ruins the image of romance.

Now, one more thing before I stop rambling. When your mother saw your letter, she turned white as a sheet. She said, "You tell her to get out of there. That is no place for a young lady." She trembled for two days. I am still not sure she's over it. Every few days she asks if I have heard from you and if you have moved yet. She knows better than to think I hide letters from her. I don't know why she is opposed to that place, but from her accent, I know she's from the south. Maybe she came from there? Do you think she is afraid that the same thing that happened to her will happen to you? Please be careful. I can't think of anything bad happening to you without crying.

Please know that we both love you. If you ever want to come for a visit, our door is always open, even if one of us won't admit that.

Lots of love,
Patty

Katie sat at the window for a long time letting images of her childhood wash over her. She thought of her mother, healthy and strong; always adamant that a woman could do anything a man could. She preached endlessly that a woman didn't need a man to survive. Katie just couldn't make her mind picture her mother any other way. She wished Patty had included a picture of her mother. Of course, that would be impossible. Katie had a ton of pictures of herself from childhood, but her mother had never allowed her own picture to be taken. This was the first time in her life that Katie began to question her mother's motives.

An arriving car caught Katie's attention. As she watched, a tall blonde got out of the driver's seat of a sporty Nissan. The woman had barely closed the car door when Michael stepped off the porch. The blonde woman threw herself into his arms and Katie could hear her laughter through the closed window. Michael returned the hug and gently set the woman back on her own feet. Taking her hand, Michael led her away from the house and out toward the fields. A few steps past the edge of the driveway, the two disappeared from view behind a line of trees. Thirty minutes later, the woman stormed back to her car. Yelling over her shoulder, Katie caught the words "you can go to hell," before the woman threw her car in reverse and tore down the lane to the street.

A few minutes later, Michael returned to the yard and glanced up to see Katie sitting at the window. He turned his face away and continued walking.

It took a while for Katie to realize that what she felt was jealousy. She didn't know if she was jealous of the interaction between Michael and the mystery woman, or if she was jealous that Michael was hugging someone else. Until that moment, it hadn't occurred to her that she wanted to be held by someone. That was a troubling thought, and one that would bear further scrutiny, but at another time.

Getting up, Katie changed clothes and got into bed. After the sleepless night before, she desperately needed some rest. As she drifted off, she wondered what it would be like to have Michael's arm around her. That night, her fantasies filled in the blanks. Katie wasn't upset; at least it kept her from dreaming about Jenny Downing.

CHAPTER TWENTY ONE

Friday morning began with gray skies. The humidity was so thick in the air that it felt like walking through soup. The forecast called for severe storms with possible tornados late in the day. The volunteers were going to go out searching first thing this morning, but would be taking a break in the afternoon for the funeral of Elaine Henderson.

The parking lot of the church was once again packed with people. The amount of food had multiplied from the day before, but the same women stood behind the tables serving it up on Styrofoam plates. Katie would bet that the diner wasn't happy with the events; they probably only had customers that weren't able-bodied enough to search, or who couldn't get off work to aid with the efforts. With the turnout at the church, that would be very few people. Lucy and Andy arrived a few minutes after Katie and Michael. After a quick conference, Andy stayed behind to assist with the coordination and to keep an eye on the people who were coming and going while Katie, Michael and Lucy each joined a search party.

For the next four hours, each party walked through the woods calling Jenny's name. They looked under every fallen tree and into every opening in the rocks along the path. There was no sign of anything amiss, nor any reply to the calls of the searchers. It was a downtrodden group of people who returned to the lot of the church. Betsy invited Katie and Michael back to her house to shower and clean up for the funeral while Father Joe invited Lucy and Andy to clean up in the rectory.

Arriving at Betsy's house, Michael let them in using the key Betsy had given him. She had stayed behind to help clean up the tables and food and told them to return the key when they got back to the church. As Katie headed toward the stairs to use the upstairs shower, Michael grabbed her arm. He quickly tilted her head to the side and Katie's breath caught in her throat. Her heart hammered as Michael lowered his face toward her. Instead of the kiss she expected, Michael said, "You have a tick in your neck. We need to get that out and make sure you don't have any more."

Michael grabbed her other arm as she instinctively raised it to brush away the tick. "Don't do that. You'll break off the head inside your neck, then you'll have to be treated at the hospital. Let's just go find some tweezers. I can take care of it."

He followed Katie upstairs and went through the medicine cabinet while Katie looked through the drawers. Finally finding tweezers, Michael used a lighter he had picked up downstairs to sterilize the ends. Once they were hot enough, he grabbed the end of the tick and quickly pulled back. The tick popped out of Katie's neck and Michael used the lighter to burn it. Dropping the dead tick in the toilet, he reached up and grabbed a towel from the shelf over the toilet. Instructing Katie to take everything off and wrap herself in the towel, he stepped from the room to let her change.

Once Katie was changed and wrapped as securely as possible in the tiny towel, she opened the door. Michael nearly swallowed his tongue at the sight of her. Knowing there was nothing under the towel didn't help matters. As their eyes made contact, he could see the nervousness in her gaze. He reached out and gently took one of her hands in his. Pulling it toward him, he finally looked down at her arm. Slowly, he ran his hand over her forearm and up to her shoulder. Turning her arm over, he ran his fingertips down the underside of her arm back to her hand. Her skin was as soft as silk and he had a difficult time releasing her first hand to reach for her second. Repeating the process, he found no other ticks on her arms. Thinking it was over, Katie started to step back from him, her every nerve twitching. Michael grabbed hold of her shoulders and when she looked up at him, he shook his head.

"Time to turn around," he said in a strangled voice. Katie did as he said and turned her back to him. "You need to lower your towel enough for me to see your back." His voice dropped off to a whisper, as if he had difficulty getting the words out. Katie took a deep breath and allowed the towel to droop until it rested on her lower back. Michael took his hands and very lightly ran them over her back, first from shoulder to shoulder and then down the center of her spine. Katie couldn't help the shiver that ran down her body, nor could she stop the goosebumps that broke out on her skin. Not finding any other ticks, Michael hesitantly raised the towel back up, but stopped Katie from moving. Dropping to his knees behind her, Michael softly touched her ankles. Katie jumped from the unexpected touch and nearly fell over. Michael grabbed her hips to steady her, then returned his hands to her ankles. As he slid his hands up her legs, her scent filled his nostrils. She smelled of the woods, very earthy, but also very feminine. As he reached her thighs, he knew he was going to have difficulty hiding his reaction to her. Stopping at the edge of the towel, he grabbed her hips once more and turned her around. Repeating the process from her ankles to her thighs without finding anything, he stood. "Make sure you check under your breasts and in the areas I couldn't see. Also, make sure you feel your scalp for any when you wash your hair," Michael said, but he was unable to make eye contact with her.

Nodding, Katie whispered, "Who's going to check you?"

"I'm experienced in checking for ticks," he replied with a crooked smile. The thought of her hands on him was too much to contemplate in the small bathroom without crossing the line with a partner that he really liked and respected. He needed to leave now before that line became blurred.

As he was about to close the door, Katie asked, "Michael, who was that woman last night?"

Only because his gaze flew up to meet hers did he see the uncertainty in her expression as he said, "No one," and closed the door, ignoring the flash of hurt in her eyes.

An hour later, Katie and Michael returned to the church. Things were strained between them and they hadn't exchanged more than a few words since leaving Betsy's house. Of course, Lucy picked up on the tension right away. As Michael went over to talk to Chief Davidson, Lucy asked, "What's up with you two?" The wiggle of her brows made it clear what she thought was up.

"Nothing." Katie wasn't about to get into that with Lucy. She didn't really know what was going on, or even what she wanted to go on with her and Michael.

"You know the whole unit is taking bets on how soon you two hook up."

"I don't sleep with my partner. It's unethical." Katie was quick to make her point. The last thing she needed was more suspicion surrounding her career. She already had more than enough trying to overcome the opinions her current bosses had. There was no way she was going to ever cross that line.

Lucy wasn't to be deterred. "Come on. It happens all the time. And with a hunk like that for a partner, I would have already jumped him."

"It happens all the time, huh? So I suppose you've hooked up with Andy?" Katie's mood was plummeting, which was saying a lot considering how low it had been when she walked into the church.

Lucy just laughed and walked over to join her partner.

The funeral began shortly thereafter. The casket was rolled in with the lid closed at the family's request. Rick Henderson came in with his two children on either side of him. The children were far from the happy kids Katie and Michael had seen a week earlier at their Aunt Evelyn's house. Evelyn and her parents entered next. Minutes later the entire church was filled with people. The Hendersons had foregone a visitation the night before so that the search could continue for Jenny Downing.

Father Joe began the funeral mass, inviting several people to come up and say a few words. Evelyn gave a speech remembering growing up with her twin; she was the only member of the family to speak. A few of the women who had been members of the church spoke about Elaine's giving spirit. Finally, the priest said a homily and the organist began playing the exiting hymn.

Throughout the service, Michael, Katie, Lucy and Andy stood around the edges of the room and surreptitiously watched the people in the crowd. After the last notes of the closing hymn echoed through the church, the parishioners stood and waited for the casket and family to precede them down the aisle. Once they were loaded into the waiting vehicles, the procession made its way across town to the cemetery.

At the cemetery, the priest blessed the burial plot and again sprinkled holy water over the coffin. As the casket was lowered into the ground, Father Joe said, "May her soul and the souls of all the faithful departed through the mercy of God rest in peace. Amen." At the final pronouncement, the skies opened up and the predicted storms arrived in full force. The parishioners began to scatter quickly, making their way to their cars, though most were already soaked through by the time they reached them. The four agents stood silently in the rain and watched everyone leave. There was one man who wanted to linger, though with a look at the agents he quickly merged into the crowds. Michael and Katie exchanged a glance and Katie began trying to follow the man. However Betsy grabbed her arm as she headed in that direction. Betsy was one of the few who had brought an umbrella.

"Dear, you will catch your death. You just share this umbrella with me and walk an old lady to her car."

Katie glanced over at Michael to let him know she had lost the guy, but Michael had seen the exchange and knew it was pointless. Turning back to Betsy, Katie asked, "Betsy, did you see that gentleman who just walked away? He was the last one to leave."

"No, I'm afraid I didn't see anyone once the rain started. I was too busy trying to wrestle this dang umbrella up. Do you think it was him?"

"No, ma'am. I'm sure it was just a concerned friend. He was just someone I haven't seen before so I was trying to put a name to him." Katie helped Betsy into her car, closed the umbrella for her and then the door. "Drive safe," she called through the window before turning and making her way to the car where Michael was waiting.

"The weather service has issued a tornado warning for Bedford and Rutherford counties. I say we call it a night and head back home before this gets any worse." Michael started the car and, without waiting for a reply, turned toward home.

CHAPTER TWENTY-TWO

By the time Katie and Michael turned into the drive leading back to the Bed & Breakfast, the rain was coming down so hard neither of them could see two inches past the windshield. They were both still soaked from the cemetery, so the dash from the car to the back door of the house became a race to see who could get inside first. Laughing, they burst through the door and were met by five pairs of eyes as the Shoulders family stopped what they were doing and turned to face them.

Caroline was the first to move. She grabbed two towels from the dryer and handed them over. "If you'll take your wet clothes off here, I'll throw them straight into the wash. No need to track up the whole house with all the dripping you're doing." Shaking her head, she turned and headed back to the table. "Do we have all the flashlights?"

Katie looked over at Michael and knew they were both thinking the same thing. There was no way she was getting undressed in front of him twice in one day. Michael opened the dryer again and dug around a bit until he found a large terrycloth bathrobe. He handed it to Katie then picked up a sheet that was on the floor to be washed in the next load. Holding his arms out with the sheet behind him and facing away from her, he shielded Katie from view so she could quickly change into the bathrobe.

"Oh, I guess I'm so used to everyone being family," Caroline said, flustered. "I didn't mean to make you uncomfortable. Please, if this is too embarrassing, go on up and change. I can mop the floors later." Caroline's face was beet red as she realized the position she had put her guest in.

"It's okay. I'm about changed. It's not the first time today I've undressed in an awkward situation." The words were out of her mouth before she thought through what she said. Michael burst out laughing, which only fueled the curiosity on Caroline's face. Not wanting to encourage the direction of Caroline's thoughts, Katie finished the thought, "We had a slight tick incident today. Luckily, there was only one." She stepped out and changed places with Michael.

"We're gathering supplies for the cellar." Ian said, using his newly learned word. "There's a tornado warning, so we have to sleep down there." The excitement in his voice was in direct contrast to the repulsion Katie experienced at his words.

"Is he serious?" she whispered to Michael. She turned to face him just as he fastened a towel around his waist. Her mouth went dry at the sight of his muscular chest, sprinkled lightly with dark hair. She couldn't seem to make her eyes stop roving over his entire body.

Shifting his weight to one foot, Michael propped his hands on his narrow hips. "Yes, he is serious. We will be sleeping together tonight." Sheer panic at his words caused Katie's eyes to fly up to meet his. She saw the humor in his eyes and knew he had phrased his response that way on purpose. "See you down there soon, Katie. Wear something warm, it can get a bit chilly." Michael stepped around her with a chuckle and disappeared up the stairs. Kevin and

Caroline were trying not to laugh as Katie followed him out of the room. She was so mortified that she didn't dare look at either of them. As soon as she reached the upper landing, she heard them both lose the battle to contain their laughter.

Half an hour later, Katie made her way downstairs to the basement. She had spent the time drying her hair and pulling on her FBI sweatsuit and thick socks. She had seen what everyone else brought, so she quickly threw together a bag with a change of clothes, a book, her case file notes, a pen and her handgun. She had kept busy so she didn't freak out over thoughts of the dirty, dark, wet basement that she would be forced to sleep in. As she reached the bottom of the stairs, she saw a large room that ran the entire length and width of the house. The walls were cinderblock, painted a bright and soothing yellow. There were bunk beds around the edges of the room with a few tables in the center holding various board games. She laughed at herself when she saw how comfortable the room was. There was even a section to the side with couches and chairs to hang out in around a fireplace. There was a television in the corner with an assortment of movies to watch, at least until the power went out.

Kevin had built a fire and everyone was gathered around sitting on the couches. Carrie had curled up on Uncle Michael's lap and was sucking her thumb, nearly asleep. They spent several hours laughing and talking. Dinner consisted of hot dogs roasted in the fire followed by s'mores. It was a cozy environment and Katie couldn't remember ever having more fun. The kids were full of ghost stories and were happy to provide jokes and updates on everyday life. At eight, the power did go out and the sound of the thunder outside penetrated down to basement.

Michael tucked a sleeping Carrie into one of the bunk beds as Tommy curled up on another, nearly asleep himself. Soon it was only Ian and the adults left around the fire.

"Miss Katie, why didn't you use the secret stairs to come down here?" Ian asked.

"I didn't know this house had secret stairs. Can you tell me about them, or are they top secret?" Katie had enjoyed Ian's humor. She wasn't entirely sure if he was being serious or if he was about to play a joke on her.

"Well, duh, if they were top secret, I wouldn't have mentioned them. There are secret stairs from here to your room. But mom put a lock on them so they could only be opened from your room. She said she didn't want us kids to be scaring any guests who stay there. And since that's the best room in the house, she always fills it first."

"Can you show me these stairs?" Katie still wasn't sure whether or not to believe him, but he had said all that with a straight face and no one was contradicting him. Ian stood up and motioned for her to follow him. He led her to the far corner and opened a door hidden in the wall panel. Sure enough, behind the panel was a set of stairs. Ian grabbed her arm as she started to go up.

"You can't go up there. There's still a tornado warning." His tone implied that he thought she was crazy to attempt to climb the stairs. They returned to the sofa and Katie asked Ian to tell her about the stairs.

"Well, in school last week we had to pick a topic in history that still applied today. So I picked the Underground Railroad. See, our house was built in 1833 by James Martin and his wife. She was a Yankee who opposed slavery and the only way she would settle in the south was if he promised never to own slaves. When the house was built, your room was for the woman of the house after she had a baby. They would stay there until the baby was a few months old. The staircase was built so that the nanny could come and go without having to go through the common areas. Even if she didn't like slavery, they did hire African Americans to help around the house and property. Any guests that came over wouldn't like having them just walking through the house. Well, they had three children by 1840 when Mr. Martin died. Mrs. Martin kept the staff to help her manage the house, the kids and the farm. Back then, the property was a lot bigger.

"There are old diaries in the library that tell the story a lot better than I can but see, about a month after Mr. Martin died, the nanny came and asked if Mrs. Martin would help her get her family safely to the North. Mrs. Martin quietly asked around and before she knew it, her house was declared a station on the Underground Railroad. See, the Underground Railroad wasn't underground or a railroad. It just meant that there were certain safe places called 'stations' along a route from the south to the north. They used railroad terms so people wouldn't know what they were talking about.

"By then, the youngest child was walking, so Mrs. Martin had one of the farm hands come hide the stairwell behind panels in the wall. That way, if anyone ever came looking for missing slaves, they had a place to hide and a way to get out without being seen." Ian finished his story with a deep breath.

Katie's eyes were as big as saucers as she looked at him. "Ian, how many stops were there in this area? Were they always houses?" Katie remembered learning about the Underground Railroad when she was younger, but in Arizona, the historical importance hadn't been as real as it seemed now that she was in the south. From what she could recall, it was just a quick chapter in a history book she had read.

"Oh, no, it wasn't always houses. Some of the most common places were churches; especially ones that were close to a waterway. It was quicker to get the escaped slaves onto boats and get them down the river. Back then people mostly traveled on foot. If you were lucky, you could travel on horseback, but the slaves were poor and didn't have horses. You couldn't get far in a day on foot, especially if you were being chased by someone on horseback."

Katie looked over at Michael. "That's how he did it," she said.

Michael looked at her confused. "That's how who did what?"

Katie stood and waved Michael to the other side of the room. She didn't want to discuss this in front of Ian. When they were a safe distance away, Katie began pacing and urgently whispering. "That's how he got Elaine Henderson out of the church. Think about it. The church is near the Duck River. There has to be a hidden tunnel under Christ the King Church. That building is much older than this house. If it *was* used as part of the Underground Railroad, it would be the perfect place to use as a station. They could have put a panel in the wall that leads to a cellar! And the cellar could have a tunnel which leads to the water!" As she talked, Katie's hands waved erratically in the air. The more she reasoned this out, the more sure she was that she was right. "Think about Barbie's description of the room she was in. She said it was an unfinished basement type room. The floor was dirt and the walls were dirt and rock. There was a staircase carved into the wall that led upward. I bet that stairway leads to a panel that opens into that back room. The columns she was chained to had to support the entire floor of the back of the church. The dimensions she gave were approximately the same as the back part of the building. It is older, so the floor joists would be different than those used today. Michael, we need to get over there. What if Jenny is in that room right now? We need to go!" Katie spun around and headed for the stairs to go up to the kitchen. Michael grabbed her arm.

"I think you're right, but we can't go out there right now. Don't you remember the rain when we got here? It is ten times worse right now. We won't do Jenny or anyone else any good if we go out and get ourselves killed."

Katie knew he was right. Leaving now wouldn't be wise. But she could no longer sit still.

The next few hours were the longest Katie could ever remember. She paced the length of the basement until Michael grabbed her arm and made her sit. Even sitting, she fidgeted, crossing and uncrossing her legs. Her thumbnail was chewed to the quick within thirty minutes. All she could do was hope that the weather was bad enough that the kidnapper hadn't had time to make it to his lair. She hoped that Jenny was alone, because alone and scared was better than what she could be going through if he had made it back to her.

The worst of the storm moved out by midnight. All the kids and Caroline and Kevin had long since fallen asleep. Katie and Michael sat by the fire. Michael couldn't help but think about how romantic the evening could have been if they both hadn't been obsessed with thoughts of what a madman might be doing. And if they weren't partners. The minute that the tornado warning expired, Katie stood up and looked at Michael. She didn't have to say a word as he stood beside her. Rushing upstairs, they both made sure they had their weapons, phones and credentials. Michael called Father Joe and asked him to meet them at the back door of the church in forty-five minutes, but not to go in until they got there. He knew that downed trees and wires could slow their progress. Once he finished that conversation, he called Chief Davidson and asked him and a few deputies to meet them at the church as well.

The rain was still coming down in sheets as they made their way to Shelbyville. There were three police cars in the lot with the Chief when they arrived. Five deputies got out of the cars and Father Joe and the Chief got out of his unmarked car. As Father Joe unlocked the door, Michael began explaining Katie's theory. Katie didn't wait to hear, she made a quick dash to the room that held the donations. The yard sale was scheduled for this morning, providing the weather cleared up.

Katie went directly to the wall behind the toy table and began feeling along the panels. It took her less than a minute to find the latch and wrench open the panel. The men were still making their way into the room.

"Katie, wait," Michael began, but she didn't listen. She disappeared down the stairs as they began winding their way through the display tables.

Reaching the bottom, the first thing Katie saw was Jenny suspended from the support beams. She had blood running down her body from some of the lashes of the whip. Her eyes were huge and filled with fear. Katie rushed forward. "Don't worry. We'll get you out of here." That was the last thing Katie remembered before everything went black.

CHAPTER TWENTY-THREE

The man had just stepped away from Jenny when he heard the creak of the panel moving from upstairs. He was standing by the wall to the left of the stairs when the female FBI agent rushed past. She never even stopped to look around. He knew she wouldn't be alone and that he had only seconds to get out of there. Grabbing the Pear of Anguish that was laying on the table, he quickly swung it up and brought it crashing down onto her head. She crumpled to the floor, unconscious. He looked at Jenny and debated cutting her down to take with him. He hadn't had a chance to finish her punishment. But the sound of footsteps making their descent shook him out of his thoughts. He turned, grabbed his clothes from the hook behind Jenny and took off running through the tunnel. He didn't have time to even stop and change. It was a good thing he always kept his boots on under the robe.

Michael entered the room and immediately saw Katie lying on the ground. Jenny looked at him, saw his gun, and quickly nodded over her shoulder, trying to communicate that he had run off behind her. It was frustrating that she couldn't talk with the iron in her mouth.

Michael quickly scanned the room, then waved the deputies down the stairs. Addressing the youngest looking officer, he said, "Stay with my partner and get medics here now." He quickly led the other officers down the tunnel after the disappearing hooded figure.

The man was too far in front of them to make out a distinct form. He was also more familiar with the tunnel and quickly added to the distance between them. By the time Michael and the officers made it to the end of the tunnel, the figure was nowhere in sight. Tom and Jerry each paired up with one of the other officers and took off in separate directions with assurances that Michael could return inside and see about the crime scene and his partner.

When Michael returned to the room, Father Joe and Chief Davidson had made their way down the stairs. Father Joe had gotten a robe from the choir room upstairs and covered Jenny. Katie was still lying on the floor, unconscious. The young deputy was nowhere to be seen.

Chief Davidson looked up from where he was kneeling beside Katie. "She's alive. Looks like he hit her with that piece of metal." He nodded to the lump a few feet away.

Michael knew immediately what it was, having seen one like it removed from Elaine Henderson's body. He didn't say this to the chief; instead, he began photographing the scene using his cell phone. He knew that if he sat down beside Katie he would reveal too much of the conflict inside him. He also knew that allowing the chief to sit with her kept him from exploring the room too closely. Five minutes later, paramedics made their way down the stairs with the young deputy and took over the care of the two ladies. One of the paramedics called Michael over. "Do you have any idea how to get this contraption off her head?" he asked, referring to Jenny.

"Katie's the expert in this, I have no idea."

"We need to clear her airway to make sure we can treat her if something happens." The medic looked perplexed and Jenny just continued to silently weep as she shivered.

Just then, Katie stirred. At first the paramedic attending to her wouldn't allow her to move. At her insistence, she finally sat up, but the room swam before her eyes. Michael quickly went over to her. "Katie, you need to lie down and let the medics do their job."

"Did we get him?" she asked, ignoring the pounding in her head and the nausea that threatened to make her vomit.

"No, we didn't. Since you're not going to be cooperative with the medic, can you tell me how to get the gag off Jenny?"

"Look for the table with his devices on it. There should be a key. Most likely it will be a screw of some kind." With that, Katie laid back down to let the dizziness pass. The paramedic took advantage of her position to quickly insert an IV into her hand.

Michael jogged over to the table against the wall and searched for something similar to what Katie described. He found a narrow screw with a flower-like head and took it over to Jenny. At the back of the metal bands, he found a hole that the screw fit into perfectly. A few twists later, the bands separated and Jenny quickly spit the gag out. Several pieces of her teeth came with it. The paramedics quickly strapped both women to backboards and began taking them up the stairs.

After Jenny was taken up, Lucy and Andy appeared in the room. "Great job, Michael. Where's Katie?" Lucy asked. She stopped in her tracks as she saw the paramedics lift Katie to follow Jenny's path upstairs.

"I need a favor," Michael said. "Can you two stay here and oversee the forensics? I need to go with Katie to the hospital." At their nod, he quickly ran upstairs, got in his car and followed the ambulance to the Bedford County Medical Center.

By the time Michael parked and made his way into the emergency entrance, Katie had been wheeled up to have a CAT scan. Because he wasn't family, the hospital staff wouldn't release information to him. Two hours later the same doctor who had treated Barbie Jones came into the waiting room. Michael jumped to his feet. He had been joined in the waiting room by SAC Nelson, who was waiting for information on her condition before calling Katie's mother. When Dr. Abrams saw Michael, he came over. "So, this time I'm treating your partner. Is this an official case?" When Michael nodded, Dr. Abrams continued, "She has a concussion so you can expect her to be dizzy and have double vision for a while. Some people complain of nausea as well. She's fussing to get out of here. If she has someone to stay with her, I will release her. If not, we'd like to keep her here for a few more hours. She needs to stay awake until her vision clears."

"I'll see that she's taken care of. She's staying in a place with a lot of people, so she *will* be monitored closely." Michael almost laughed at how closely she would be watched. Caroline wouldn't let her have a moment's peace until she was sure Katie was alright.

"Oh, one more thing," the doctor said, "She asked that you not call her emergency contact for a small bump on the head. Said she doesn't want to worry anyone unnecessarily." With that, he led the two agents down the hall to the small cubicle where Katie lay.

Katie's face was pale under her tan complexion and she had a large knot forming on the side of her head, but she was alert and giving the nurse orders to remove her IV line. When they rounded the corner, Katie turned her attention to the doctor. "Please tell her to let me out of here. I have a case to solve. What do we know about Jenny Downing's condition? Is she alert?" Katie was already reaching for her credentials and her weapon, which had been put on the bedside table. As she stood up, she quickly reached out to grab the edge of the bed to steady herself.

"Agent Freeman, I will release you provided you go with your partner and take it easy." His stern look was wasted on Katie.

"Of course I'm going with Agent Powell. We're in the middle of an investigation."

The doctor shook his head. "Investigating is not taking it easy."

The mulish expression that came across her face was plain to everyone. "We have someone out there abducting and torturing women. You have now treated two of those victims. Do you really think I can go put my feet up and watch a chick flick while eating ice cream when I know we just seriously pissed this guy off? I promise I won't do anything stupid, like running into a dark cellar before checking to see if it's clear. Right now, I want to get up and I want to go talk to Jenny Downing. That isn't too strenuous, is it?" The fact that her hand hadn't left the butt of her holstered weapon made the doctor think twice about how many restrictions he should put on her.

Turning to Michael, the doctor said, "Try to keep her calm and don't let her chase anyone. Make her sit as much as possible. She doesn't need to be crawling around on the ground looking for evidence either - nothing more strenuous than walking, talking and sitting. Jenny Downing is three curtains down." With that, Dr. Abrams walked out of the room.

"You didn't call my mother, did you?" Katie asked their boss.

"No, not yet. I was waiting until I had more information. If you had been unconscious, I would have already called. Michael assured me that this was just a bump on your head. From what your old SAC told me, that shouldn't hurt too much." Laughing at his own joke, Nelson turned and left the room with a caution to both of them about wrapping up this investigation before anyone else was injured.

They met up with Dr. Abrams in the hall as he stepped out of Jenny's room. Holding her file, he motioned them away from the curtain. "I've made sure no one asked her questions or told her anything about what's happened. There are two small circular burn marks just above her hip on her lower back. My opinion is that he used a stun gun to subdue her. She has the same marks and bruises as Barbie Jones, consistent with the same instrument. Only hers are more numerous and several broke the skin. Only one mark required stitches, the rest we just cleaned and put salve on. There is no evidence of rape, though she told us that before we examined her. She is dehydrated and hungry. We have her hooked to saline and are giving her broth for now. She also has chipped and broken teeth, just like Mrs. Jones."

Thanking the doctor for the information, they entered the curtained area to find Betsy holding Jenny's hand. Though her eyes were closed, the tears leaking out the sides indicated that she was awake. Katie nodded to Michael to begin the questions.

Michael cleared his throat and when Jenny looked up, he introduced himself and Katie. "Would you mind answering a few questions for us?"

Jenny licked her lips and reached for the cup of ice water beside her bed. "Thank you for finding me," she said. Her voice was raspy and her eyes again filled with tears. When she had collected herself, she nodded for them to ask any questions they had.

Pulling up a chair, Michael took her other hand while Katie stood at the foot of the bed. Chief Davidson stepped into the room and pulled the curtain closed behind him. He nodded hello at the women, then shook his head at the agents to let them know they hadn't caught the guy. Michael turned back to Jenny. "Are you okay with Betsy being in here? We can ask anyone that you're not comfortable speaking in front of to step out." He looked apologetically toward Betsy, but saw only understanding in her eyes.

"I'm fine with her here. She's more of a mother to me than I have ever had." Again, Jenny had to take a minute to compose herself, so did Betsy.

"Why don't you start from the beginning and just tell us what you remember. Once you're done, I'll ask questions to fill in the blanks or to clarify something. OK?"

Jenny took a deep breath. "I remember Betsy and I leaving the room at the church Wednesday night. The nurse told me it's Saturday now. It sure felt like I was in that room longer than two days." She shook her head and took another sip of water.

"I went out to my car, but it wouldn't start. I remember someone knocking on my window. I jumped because it scared me. But then everything goes blank. I don't know if I got out or why I can't remember." She looked to Michael to see if he had the answer.

"There are marks on your lower back toward the left hip that indicate he used a stun gun on you." Michael was very matter of fact without giving too much detail. He didn't want to fill in the blanks for her, but given the location of the marks, she probably never even knew what hit her.

Nodding, Jenny went on with her story. "When I woke up, I was tied to the posts where you found me. I was trying to get loose when I first felt the sting from the whip." Jenny gently squeezed Betsy's hand as the older woman gasped. Obviously Jenny had been covered up before Betsy came into the room.

"He kept hitting me from behind for a long time. Then he came around and started on the front." Here she paused, thinking back. "I think he said something. Hmmm… Yes, he said I had committed adultery. I tried to tell him he was wrong. See Jack is the one who was sleeping around. I got tired of it, and his drinking, and left. I've been talking a lot to Melissa and Tiffany, they're Jack's former wives. They tried to stop me from marrying him, but I was a stupid eighteen-year-old who knew everything. Anyway, he kept hitting me for a long time. I was about to pass out when he finally stopped. Then he-" Jenny had to pause again. Taking a few sips of water and even more deep breaths, she continued.

"He washed me off. There was something in the water. It smelled nice, but it stung a bit when it hit the areas with broken skin. Oh, and he was chanting. Something from Psalms, but he changed the words. I only remember the part about being crushed and broken. It was like he was forewarning me. I guess that doesn't make much sense, but I had a really bad feeling about those words."

Right then a nurse came in to check her vital signs and change the saline bag hanging from the pole beside her bed. Once she had gone, Michael asked, "What did he do after he washed you?"

Jenny was quiet for a while with her head laid back and her eyes closed. Finally, she looked up, "He untied me and took me over to the table in the room. Then he tied my arms and legs down. I thought for sure he would rape me, but all he did was tell me that he would be back. He said 'we'll try again in the morning.' I don't know what he wanted from me." Tears were again running down Jenny's face.

"Do you need a break? We can come back later," Michael offered.

"I would prefer to get this over with now, if you don't mind," Jenny replied. "I was there for a long time. It hurt laying on that wooden table. My back was on fire from his whip and if I tried to move to get comfortable, I felt the wood dig into my skin. It's funny, I thought maybe I would get a splinter and die from the infection before he could do anything worse to me. Then I thought of my kids. I didn't want to die. If I die, there isn't anyone left who would love my kids." At this, she broke down in heaving sobs. Betsy gathered her up and murmured soft words of comfort to her, but when she tried to rub Jenny's back, Jenny gasped and pulled away. Collecting herself, Jenny smiled her thanks at Betsy.

"When he came back, he tied me to the posts again. I tried to fight him, but he was very strong. I did get a close up look at his eyes through the hood. They were blue and I swear they were familiar. He smelled like whiskey. He repeated the same thing as the time before. He just kept hitting me, then he would come around to the front of me and start all over. When I would begin to pass out, he would stop for a while. He would get his breath back. As he paced, he would say scripture, and then he would curse himself and me. He kept telling me that I should stop tempting him with my nakedness. That another man's wife shouldn't behave that way. I wanted to tell him to give my clothes back and I would cover myself, but I couldn't talk. He never took that thing out of my mouth. I was so thirsty." As if that were a reminder, she reached again for the cup of water. "He went through about three cycles of using the whip that time with pauses to let me recover. Once, he waved ammonia under my nose to make sure I was awake.

"When he was done, he tied me to the table again and left. The next thing I remember was hearing the rain. I knew I wasn't too far underground if I could hear the thunder and rain. I saw a few flashes of light from the direction where he came and went. I laid there listening to the rain and praying my boys were safe. I prayed that I would see them again. He came shortly after the rain started and tied me to the posts again. I didn't have the energy to fight him that time. I knew what was coming and just prayed that I could take it until I was found. He had just finished his second round of beatings when I saw you come down the stairs," her gaze shifted to Katie. "I thought I was hallucinating. And then you charged right past him. I wanted to scream at you to turn around, but he hit you on the head and you went down. I thought for sure we were both dead after that. But then I heard more footsteps on the stairs and he bolted. I suppose you know the rest."

Katie gently touched her foot. "You did well. You will get through this. We won't ask you any questions for now. Get some sleep and if there is anything we can do for you, please let us know. If you remember anything else before we come back, please call us." Katie placed her business card on the table beside the bed and the two agents left the room to let Jenny rest.

CHAPTER TWENTY-FOUR

It was just after four in the morning when they finished with Jenny, and Michael insisted that they stop for something to eat. Making their way to the little diner on Church Street that had served them well over the past few days, they grabbed a corner booth. It was early yet for the breakfast crowd, but the coffee was already hot and strong. Michael ordered a breakfast that would feed an army while Katie ordered an omelet with ham and cheese and her usual sweet tea, not coffee.

Michael wanted nothing more than to go catch a few hours of sleep, but knowing Katie couldn't sleep with a concussion and that there was a madman out there made him push on. "By the way, you're getting pretty good at talking with people. For someone who claims to have no social skills, I think you're coming along fine under my tutelage." Michael gave a rakish grin. "So what are your thoughts? I know something is going on in your mind. You had too much time to think while lying in that bed. What's your theory?"

Amused that he already knew her so well, Katie said, "I want to go back to the church. I didn't get to look around in the lair. I need a better feel for this guy before I can say for sure. I think Jenny is right. This guy was familiar with her and she knows him. Does this mean that he was targeting her from the beginning, or does he know all three of our victims? From her story and the limited time Barbie spent with him, I think he has a god-complex."

"He definitely has difficulty with women. I mean, stripping a woman naked and then punishing her for revealing herself to him? That is definitely a problem. I'm thinking he had a wife who cheated. Maybe he looks for other women who are cheating and is punishing them," Michael added.

Katie carefully considered him as she thought that over. "It would seem that way if you only consider Elaine and Jenny. Elaine was having repeated dinners with a man who was not her husband. No one knew it was her brother. He accused Jenny of having an affair. I wonder where he got that notion? We need to ask Jenny that. But when you think of Barbie, that theory doesn't hold. He accused her of killing children. Maybe it isn't the cheating, but any fault with a woman that he needs to punish. Still doesn't explain how he knew about Barbie's miscarriages. If he were Father Joe, that would be plausible, but we already know it wasn't him." They stayed and debated the different aspects of the case as Michael finished his breakfast. After paying the check, they headed back to Christ the King church.

Andy greeted them at the door to the back hallway. "Welcome back, Agent Freeman. Guess your head is harder than it looks, or maybe all that hair cushioned the blow?" Andy laughed at his own joke. "If you need any TLC, just let me know. My house is always available." He quickly moved on, seeing the look on Michael's face.

"This place is incredible. You have to come check it out. There are all sorts of internal passageways." He led them back to the panel in the yard sale room. The weather had cleared, so the deputies had carried the tables out to the far side of the parking lot. With the events of the night before, the yard sale had almost been canceled, but, everyone agreed it could go on as long as no one was allowed into the building. The sale promised to be a huge success. The events of the previous night were sure to draw an even bigger crowd than originally expected.

Andy continued his dialog as they went down the stairs. Katie finally held up her hand to stop him. Michael hid the smile as Andy stopped mid-sentence. Michael knew that Katie liked to form her own opinions and she was already mad that she had missed most of the evidence collection due to her own stupidity.

The first place she headed was the wooden table to the left. Just as Barbie had said, when tied to the posts it would have been on her right. On the table, the evidence technicians had bagged all the metal items. She saw another Scavenger's Daughter and a Pear of Anguish. The Scold's Bridle that had been around Jenny's head had also been bagged as evidence. The number of footprints in the dirt floor showed the amount of traffic that had passed through the space. Michael, Lucy and Andy just stood back and watched Katie work. Katie slowly made her way around the room. Lights had been set up in the corners to illuminate the room more than the oil lantern the perpetrator had used. When she had seen all that she needed to, Katie turned and headed down the tunnel.

"We haven't put lights in there yet. You might want to grab a flashlight," the nearest technician said.

He handed a long-handled black flashlight to her. Switching it on and saying thanks, Katie headed down toward the water she could hear rushing by at the end. Michael quickly joined her, not wanting to let her out of his sight. They didn't speak as she directed the beam all around. She made sure to illuminate the path ahead, but she also examined the walls and floor to the left and right of them. There was nothing of interest as they emerged in the woods a few feet from the bank of the Duck River.

"Shit, I know exactly where we are," Katie said. "I passed here twice with two different search parties." She turned and went back down the tunnel to see what else she had missed. "Andy, continue...please." The last was added as she realized how harsh she sounded.

"Oh, I would rather show you," he said.

"You've been working with perverts for far too long." Katie muttered as she followed him up the dirt and rock stairs.

Before they exited through the panel back into the room that once held the yard sale items, Andy pointed to his right. He turned to see the expression on Katie's face as she saw the gap between the wall to the exterior room and the original wall of the structure. "There is about a foot of space behind every exterior wall in this part of the church. Go ahead, see for yourself." He stepped aside and waved Katie through.

As Katie walked through, she occasionally saw shafts of light coming from the other side. She touched one of the squares highlighted along the edges with light. There was a sliding panel that she quickly pushed aside. Looking through a space about the size of her eye, she saw into the women's restroom. Closing it, she moved along to the next one. She slid aside each square she passed and discovered a view of the room beyond. Behind the final hidden panel, she discovered the confessional. Her eye was directly behind where the priest's head would be when he heard someone's confession. Katie turned to go back toward the exit when she came face-to-face with Andy. He had a smirk on his face, knowing that this discovery was very important.

"Oh, don't look so smug. I was the one who figured out there were hidden panels," Katie said in a playfully snippy voice. Andy just rolled his eyes and reached past her to push another lever. A large portion of the inside of the confessional slid to the side and he made an "after you" gesture for Katie to step out first. Andy chuckled as he watched her try to hide the awe of this discovery.

The two of them walked down the hall in the interior of the church and joined Michael and Lucy, who had come up from the basement. Father Joe and Chief Davidson were also in the back room. "Does anyone know when these walls were built?" Katie addressed Father Joe in particular.

"The church was renovated about three years ago. The original interior was built to have exposed rock walls. This section was added on to the main church in the 1800's. Back then it was a Baptist church. Christ the King took over in the 1940's and as we grew, we used this back section more and more. We discovered that it wasn't insulated well enough. The rooms were freezing in the winter, though pleasantly cool in the summer. It got so cold in here one winter that we couldn't have our activities anymore. So my predecessor, Father Nicholas, collected the money and had the renovation done. The walls were built in a foot so that we could put sufficient insulation behind them, or so I thought.

"We need to know who did the renovation to the church, Father. Do you have those records?"

"Of course, come with me." Father Joe went back down the hall and turned in to his office. It took about ten minutes of flipping through file cabinets, but he finally came up with correct folder. "It was a company called Restoration and Renovation Contractors, or R&R Contractors; their logo is a person sleeping. Rather ingenious, I think." He handed the folder to Katie.

Katie flipped through the folder quickly then handed it to Lucy who took digital photos and passed the original back to Father Joe. They quickly said their goodbyes, promising to be in touch with anything they discovered, and headed out. SAC Nelson waited for them by the door to the parking lot. "Agent Freeman, you've done enough for today. Agents Boggs and Dillon will take the information about the renovation and cross check the employee records with anyone you've crossed paths with in this investigation. Any connections can be followed up on later. Unless there is another abduction, you are to return home and have nothing to do with this case until Monday morning. Agent Powell, you've put in too many long hours as well. I'm ordering you to see that neither you nor Agent Freeman touch this case until then, understood?" He waited for Michael's nod before he got in his car and drove off.

Andy and Lucy wisely retreated as quickly as they could before Katie could turn her temper on anyone nearby. She was livid to be ordered home like an invalid. She had worked longer hours than this before. True, none of those hours had involved a concussion, but still, she was perfectly functional. As she turned to quickly to voice her anger at Michael, the world started spinning again and she would have fallen if he hadn't caught her arm in time to steady her.

"That is what he meant. You are still deathly pale and you need to eat again. I'm taking you home and you *are* going to rest this afternoon. Perhaps if you get some sleep, I can talk him into lifting the ban tomorrow. Right now there is nothing you can do other than run yourself ragged. And that isn't helping anyone." Michael dragged her to the car, opened the passenger door and gently pushed her inside.

CHAPTER TWENTY-FIVE

The weekend was very quiet. They returned to the house and were served lunch in the sunroom. Katie was entertained by the kids, who were finally out of school for the year. June was quickly approaching and the weather after the rain was beautiful for sitting on the porch. At two, Carrie curled up on Katie's lap and half an hour later Michael found them sitting in the porch swing, both fast asleep. He gently extricated Carrie from Katie's arms and carried her upstairs. He then returned and carried Katie up to her room and laid her on the bed, covering her with the quilt.

Katie slept until nearly noon the next day and probably would have slept longer if her stomach and bladder had held out. She made her way downstairs and found Michael sitting at the kitchen table with Caroline. Today, he was wearing dark jeans and a lime-green polo.

Katie helped herself to a glass of sweet tea from the refrigerator. Caroline took her elbow and guided her to a seat. "Sit down, honey, and I'll get you something to eat." She began bustling around the kitchen putting together a tray of deli meat and cheese. She brought them to the table with hoagie rolls and assorted condiments.

"Have we heard from Lucy and Andy?" Katie began piling her roll with meat. Michael waited for her to finish before he began making his own sandwich.

"Yes. We received an email from them a few hours ago. I came over to see if you had seen it yet. I was just debating with Caroline on whether or not we should wake you up. How's your head?"

Katie waved off his concern. "I'm fine. What's in the email?"

"Sorry, but you have to finish your sandwich before we talk business." Michael smiled, but his eyes were serious. Katie rolled her eyes and took a giant bite.

"Mom says it isn't nice to stuff your mouth," Tommy said. Michael nearly choked on the bite in his mouth as he laughed. Katie just smiled.

"Okay, now that you're fed, Lucy's report matched three names from the payroll of R&R Construction to people who still live in Shelbyville. She sent those names along for us to investigate and is going to run quick checks on the others just to make sure we don't miss anything. First up is John Clark. He was employed at R&R for five years, but moved on to start his own business. On paper, he seems like a great guy. Married, two kids, another on the way. No record, not even a traffic ticket. Second is Paul Dennis. I find him interesting. He still works at R&R, has for about fifteen years. He has one arrest for smoking weed. No wife or kids, but he appears to be dating Claudette. I could see how that would cause issues with women." Michael chuckled at his own joke. "Finally, we have Timothy Owens. Background check shows two children, but no mention of a wife. He too is a long-term employee of R&R." As he spoke, he handed each person's sheet to Katie.

"Timothy Owens sound familiar. How do we know that name?" Katie stared at the picture of Owens from his driver's license. Something tickled her brain as she looked but she couldn't place him. There was nothing in his check that set off any bells.

"I don't recall that name coming up in our investigation. He doesn't look familiar to me, either." Michael took a second look but just shook his head.

Pulling out her notes, Katie reviewed all the interviews but nothing stood out. Finally, she said, "I say we go talk to these guys. Today might be best because it's Sunday. They likely aren't working so we should find them at home."

"You're forgetting we're on vacation until tomorrow."

She was already shaking her head before Michael could get the sentence out. "I have rested, eaten and recovered. I am no longer dizzy or seeing double. I am not about to sit here and do nothing all day while this guy could be planning his next abduction or scouting out a site to keep his next victim." Katie was indignant. She all but stood up and put her hands on her hips.

Michael couldn't stop the smile that spread across his face. "Alright, let's go then."

They pulled up in front of the Clark residence and watched John playing in the front yard with two boys approximately ten and twelve years old. They were throwing a football back and forth. After watching for a few minutes, they both got out and went to talk to him.

"Afternoon, Mr. Clark. Do you have a few minutes?" Michael asked after showing Clark his credentials.

"What's this about? Boys, why don't you run in and get something to drink?" John turned his attention back to the agents. He appeared confused, but not worried or nervous.

"You used to work for R&R Construction, didn't you?"

Clark nodded. I worked there for about five years. I've made the rounds of different construction companies so I could hone my skills. Once I felt I was proficient enough, I opened my own business." John relaxed at the question. He still had no idea what was going on, but was open in his answers.

"Were you part of the team that renovated Christ the King Church?"

Nodding, John said, "That was the biggest job the company did the whole time I was employed there. Took a good six or eight months to complete."

"What part of the renovation did you handle?" Michael was trying to gauge his personality by asking the easy questions first.

"Well, I was part of the crew that dismantled what was already in the room. It wasn't much actually. The space was one big open room when we started and it didn't have anything over the rock on three of the walls. Where the addition had been added to the existing structure, there was some old framing. We had to be careful that when we took it down we didn't cause any damage to the older main building and that we had enough support for the roof of the newer structure. I was only there for about two or three weeks of the project, right at the beginning. I did go back when it was finished just to see what the inside looked like."

"So you don't attend church there?" Katie interjected.

"No, ma'am, my wife and I are Baptist. I know lots of folks that go there, though. I knew Elaine Henderson. Terrible, what happened to her." Again, he was very matter of fact.

Katie knew he wasn't their guy after just these few minutes, but she needed to make sure. Deciding to cut to the chase, she asked, "Where were you the night Elaine disappeared?"

John was struck speechless. He stared at her with his mouth hanging open. "You seriously think I'm responsible for those three women? I didn't even know Elaine was missing until I got home from vacation. My family was in Florida for the week when she disappeared. I was working overtime when the Jones woman disappeared. I was trying to make up for the time off. When you own your own business, you don't have the luxury of paid vacations. As for the Downing woman, I was home with my family that night. We got a call from our neighbors and I went out to help search." John's quiet demeanor had changed, his body language now rigid as he spoke.

Nodding, Katie said, "Thank you for being so forthcoming." She turned to walk away as Michael shook hands and thanked him for his time, explaining that they were asking these questions of anyone who was working at R&R when the renovation occurred. John just nodded and turned to join his kids inside, still upset over the questions.

Michael got behind the wheel of the car and blasted the air conditioning. "I think I have to take back what I said about your people skills. Why the need to be so brisk back there?" He frowned at Katie as he pulled the car out onto the street.

"You know as well as I do that he wasn't our guy. I just wanted to hurry things along. We don't have time to spend with all three of these men, especially if none of them are who we're looking for. I think Paul Dennis will take the longest, he seems the most likely on paper, and dating a domineering woman like Claudette can really mess with a guy's mind." Katie didn't apologize for her brisk manner. She just looked forward out the windshield waiting for Michael to arrive at Paul's house.

The house they pulled up to was in desperate need of repair. It appeared to have once been green, but the paint was chipping and peeling and more of the grayish under layer showed than the actual paint. The front steps were solid, having been recently replaced, but the railing was badly attached and would probably have blown down in a good gust of wind.

Paul Dennis was a shrimp of a man. He stood barely five and a half feet tall and couldn't have weighed more than 130 pounds. His jet black hair was a bit too long and he wore it slicked straight back. His large, hawk-like nose was his biggest visible feature. When Michael introduced them, Paul's eyes became shifty. "I ain't got no weed on me. I gave that shit up a long time ago man. You got no right coming here."

Exchanging glances, Michael stepped back to let Katie take over. They both instinctively knew that a tough female would get more information from Paul than Michael's nice-guy questioning. Katie stepped forward and got as close to Paul as she could. She was a good three or four inches taller. In a low, firm voice, she asked, "Where were you Wednesday night?"

Paul visibly paled. "I wasn't nowhere," Paul stammered. He tried to close the door, but Katie blocked it with a firm slap of her palm, which caused him to flinch back.

"Try again, Paul. We know you were at the church. People saw you." Katie had half her body inside the door at this point. She couldn't legally go any further unless he invited them in.

"Ain't no one saw me there. I was careful to stay hidden." Paul gave a smug smile, which slowly faded as Katie let a silence hang in the air. It took him a full minute to realize what he said. "Wait a minute," he stammered, "you can't blame Jenny's disappearance on me! I was there, yes, but just 'cause I needed to see if Claudette was there. She's been tellin' me that she's gonna leave me. Said she could find better. I just needed to see if she was really there or not. I saw Jenny leave and go to her car. But Claudette came out right after. I was too busy watching her to pay attention to Jenny. Claudette got in her car and I had to run back to mine. I tried to catch up with Claudette, but she's a fast driver. By the time I made it to my car, she was long gone. I drove to her daddy's house and parked on the street. Her daddy don't like me none too much. I had to sneak on the property. Nearly got my leg chewed off by that damn beast of a dog. Luckily he smelled me first and knew I was no harm. Claudette was in the house already. I watched for a little bit and then came home."

"I think you need to come with us." Katie signaled to Michael, who stepped away to call Chief Davidson and let him know they were bringing in Paul Dennis. "We're going to take a little ride down to the police station and get this story of yours on video."

Paul began shaking. "I don't wanna go downtown. They ain't very nice to me." He looked everywhere but at Katie or Michael.

"You can come with us now, or I can handcuff you and send for a squad car. Personally, I think they'll treat you a bit nicer if you come on your own." Katie's voice was steel. She left no room for him to turn down the offer. Finally, his shoulders slumped and he slid his feet into the tiny flip flops by the door and stepped out. He was in a ratty white sleeveless t-shirt and cut-off blue jeans and his arms looked no bigger around than the spindles that made up the flimsy railing.

After placing Paul in the backseat, Michael touched Katie's arm to get her attention. "He doesn't seem to fit our crime. Why are we taking him in? I respect your opinion, but you usually read people better. Damned if I know how you do it, but he just doesn't seem right for this."

Katie rubbed her toe in circles on the ground and swiped her hand to smooth her hair back, though it was still encased in her usual bun. After thinking a few minutes, she looked up at Michael. "I grew up on a ranch. The only ones who came on and off the property were a few trusted people, like the doctor, or the lawyer, or the woman who ran the women's shelter; and then there were the women and children that we housed. Mom has a soft spot for helping the less fortunate, especially those trying to get out of an abusive situation. When all you are around are damaged people, you learn to recognize certain body language: when someone is afraid, when they're in pain, when they are lying or avoiding a certain topic. I've been trained in body language my entire life. When you are a lonely little girl, you make up games to keep yourself occupied. I used to do that with the women and their daughters who came to stay with us.

"I know Paul isn't the person who's doing this. He isn't strong enough and I don't think he's evil enough. But I want to take him in for two reasons: first, I want him to provide the alibi for Claudette. I want it officially in the record so we have something besides my instinct to clear her. Second, I think he's up to something else. I get the feeling that peeping through Claudette's window is the least of his crimes. I think we should drop him off and let the Chief and his men get alibis for the other nights that women disappeared. I think he'll have to admit to other crimes in order to clear his name on this one. Besides, if we allow the locals to interview him it will look better for future collaboration." Katie gave her cheeky grin as she finished. Michael just chuckled and shook his head.

Fifteen minutes later, they deposited Paul with Chief Davidson and explained that they wanted to keep looking for other avenues and asked if he could spare some men for the interrogation. Katie recommended a tough female for the task, which the Chief scoffed at, but finally caved and brought in one of his female officers to see to the duty. Katie spoke privately with her, outlining Paul's personality and the best way to approach him, then the two left to talk to Timothy Owens.

When no one answered the door at the Owens's house and none of the neighbors admitted to seeing him that day, Michael pulled rank and decided to call it a day. Katie needed more rest, her complexion had already returned to the pasty white it had been when they left the hospital.

Before heading back to the B&B, Katie asked to swing by the church one more time. She removed the panel in the wall and went back down to the hidden room and then followed the tunnel to the river. Michael followed her, aiming the flashlight along their path. When they reached the end of the tunnel, Katie took the light and began scanning the ground around the tunnel's exit. Finally, the light came to rest on a pile of leaves and branches. Asking Michael to hold the light, she carefully examined the pile and then lifted one branch. All the other branches lifted with it and expanded outward until the pile became almost a blanket of intertwined branches and leaves. Raising her eyebrows, Katie and Michael gathered the whole pile and brought it back with them to the car.

Chief Davidson called Katie's phone as they were about to pull out of the church lot. Smirking, Katie answered, "Hello, Chief. What can I do for you?"

Her tone had Michael shaking his head in bemusement.

"The Chief would like us to come by the station before we pack it in," Katie said as she ended the call. "I guess Paul turned out to be as interesting as I figured. This should be enlightening."

The first thing out of Chief Davidson's mouth when they walked into his office was, "You never thought he was the right guy, did you?" Though his tone was amused, he still looked a bit cross at having been mislead.

"Of course not. He isn't big enough to carry around the women who disappeared. But I knew he was up to something. I also knew that whatever it was, it would be a relief to you to get the case closed. I doubted that whatever he was up to had gone unnoticed." Katie was straightforward and unapologetic in her reply. "Are you going to tell us what he was doing?" She finally smiled at the last comment. It was obvious she was interested in knowing.

"Turns out our little peeping tom was a bit more hands-on. We've had a series of break-ins lately. It came to our attention when Officer Fuller's girlfriend mentioned that some of her undergarments were missing. At first he brushed it off because she tends to shop so much. But she insisted that a certain pair she had worn on their last date was missing. Apparently they were memorable, because he helped search for them. They were nowhere. Well, she mentioned it to a few friends and they all admitted they were missing underwear too. Officer Fuller filed a report and sure enough all the women had marks of forced entry on their bedroom windows. Seems the only time the underwear went missing was the day after each woman had a date they brought home. Our little perv only took panties with the woman's scent on them, if you get my meaning.

"The last woman who reported missing underwear came the night Elaine was taken. It appears our panty thief escalated. He knew she was alone, so he snuck in her window, took the panties, but apparently couldn't keep his hands to himself. He copped a feel of her breast, which woke her up. She screamed and he jumped out the window and fled. She called us. Guy was wearing a mask and gloves. There was no evidence to trace to anyone. Now, Paul has admitted to taking the panties. We found all of them in his house. He admitted all this because he doesn't see anything wrong with taking other women's panties. Didn't think it was a big deal. At least not compared to murdering a poor woman.

"Oh, and Agent Freeman, you were right about needing a strong female to interrogate him." The last bit was said in a strangled voice. The Chief did not like admitting that a woman could do a better job of interrogating a suspect than a man.

Choosing not to rub salt in the wound, Katie nodded and asked if Officer Fuller was still around. Chief Davidson paged him and a few minutes later, Tom entered the room.

"Officer Fuller, could you come look at something for us?" Michael asked. Both Tom and the Chief followed them to the car. Michael opened the trunk and he and Katie pulled out the tangle of branches. "Ever seen anything like this?" Michael asked.

Tom knelt down and spread the branches out so the full camouflage blanket was stretched out. It covered the length of several parking spaces. Tom went over it section by section, occasionally lifting leaves or branches for a closer look underneath. Finally he looked up. "This is the Owens family method of concealing themselves. Where did you find this?"

Katie's heart nearly beat out of her chest. "This was the covering on the exterior entrance to the tunnel. How are you sure that this belongs to the Owens family?"

"Ma'am, we have competitions every year to see who can build the best deer hunting blind." At Katie's confused expression, he explained. "A blind is where you hide yourself from the wildlife so you have a better chance of getting a kill. The better hidden you are, the closer the animals will come to you. The Owenses always win the competition hands down. They never let anyone close enough to inspect the weaving close-up, though. I used to be friends with Tim Owens and he let me see it once. I was fourteen. His daddy wore the hide off him when he found out. I tried for years to duplicate it, but I never could. Being so young and only getting a quick look, it was impossible to remember every curve and tie. Are you entering this as evidence?" Young Tom's face was glowing with excitement. The agents knew that he would study every inch of the woven mass before logging it.

At their nod, Tom gently and reverently folded the mass of branches and carried it to the back of the police station. He closed the door to the conference room and the shades so no one else could see in. Next year, the Owenses wouldn't be the winners of that competition.

The agents followed the Chief back to his office. They told him that the only person they hadn't been able to reach was Tim Owens and that he was definitely of interest. Asking the Chief about the family, they learned the entire family history.

"Well, Old Man Owens, name was Owen Owens, can you imagine doing that to a child? Well, he was a blacksmith. Worked for the big horse farm up Route 16. He was a skilled man. He forged all the shoes for the horses, bridles, bits, you name it. If a horse needed it, Owen could do it. He won competitions for his workmanship and the reputation of the farm had a lot to do with the intricacy of the beauty of the horses' dressing. Owen and his wife had four boys. I always thought Linda wanted a girl, but she died birthing the last boy, so she never got her chance. Owen, he didn't take too well to being a single parent. His oldest was eight when the youngest was born. That boy pretty much raised the other three.

From what I hear, Owen was strict. He didn't take no sass and he kept those boys in line. Trained all of them to follow in his footsteps, but only the second boy was interested. He's still out working on the farm. The older boy moved away. Last I heard, he was a lawyer or something in Nashville. Never did see the attraction of the big city. Anyway, the third boy is an architect, also in Nashville. Neither of them ever comes home. The youngest is Tim. He was a handful from the beginning. Colicky as a baby, threw the biggest tantrums as a toddler. Always did everything in his power to undermine Owen's authority. He graduated high school and moved to town, got started in construction. Seems a pretty steady lad now. Works when he's supposed to, doesn't get out much since his wife and baby died. Sent his kids to live with their oldest uncle in Nashville when the accident happened. Seems the oldest boy's wife couldn't have kids, so they welcomed the chance to raise them. Tim just couldn't seem to look at those boys once their momma was dead."

Katie had leaned forward in her seat as the chief talked. The look of excitement on her face showed she had made a connection to something else in the abduction investigation. "Chief, was Tim's wife Lily Owens? The woman Jack Downing killed?" Michael's eyebrows shot up. He had completely forgotten about the mention of that accident. Claudette had gloated about it the night Jenny disappeared.

When the chief nodded, Katie asked to see the metal pieces that had been collected from the room under the church.

"Well now, our evidence room is in the basement of the courthouse. We can't access that until morning," Chief Davidson said. Seeing Katie was about to erupt, Michael took her arm and made arrangements with the Chief to meet him at eight in the morning at the courthouse.

CHAPTER TWENTY-SIX

Katie was piping mad when they got in the car to head back to Smyrna. "The evidence is right there. We need to get into the courthouse and prove that it's him." Michael let her rant for a few minutes until she finally settled down.

"It's eight at night. We can go home, lay out all that we know, make a timeline and get a few things organized. We can discuss why you want to go see the iron pieces and what we need to look for in order to identify them to a specific maker. There are things we can do before going off half-cocked and getting one of us hurt again." Michael's quiet, reasoning voice calmed Katie a little, but she took offense at him bringing up her mistake of running into an uncleared room. They finished the ride in silence.

When they got home, they did exactly as Michael suggested. They commandeered the office and spread out the case files on the table. Andy and Lucy joined them, having booked overnight rooms so they could stay close and be part of the action the next day. Lucy began by researching Owen Owens and all that the horse world had to say about him. There was a documentary done on him when he retired which demonstrated his style of iron working and how he personalized each piece. Linder Owens, the son who had taken over for him, was part of the documentary and talked about how he altered the process and the ways he had changed the signature he put on his pieces. By the end of the documentary, all four agents were staring at the computer screen with rapt attention.

At ten, Caroline came in with a tray of cheeses and crackers and various sodas, with a glass of sweet tea for Katie. She let them all know that the house was locked and alarmed for the night and that everyone else was going to bed. At midnight, the agents called it a night and headed up to bed themselves.

Ten minutes before eight the next morning, all four agents converged on the steps of the courthouse. Fifteen minutes later, the Chief pulled in with Tom Fuller. The six of them made their way through security and down to the basement. Tom unlocked the cage doors and they all signed in. Removing the boxes labeled for the investigation, they took it through to the room in the back, which held long steel tables with bright lighting. It reminded Katie of the autopsy suite where Elaine had been taken.

Without breaking the seal on any of the bags, each agent picked a bag and began examining it through the clear plastic. Chief Davidson and Officer Fuller stood to the side, watching. The seconds stretched into minutes as each agent searched for anything to identify as Tim Owens's signature. They looked in the places the documentary had mentioned, though the closest item to anything horse related was the Scold's Bridle. None of them found a signature, even after exchanging the pieces between themselves.

Katie began pacing, gnawing an already raw thumbnail. The others explained to the chief and Tom what they were looking for. They jumped in with fresh eyes to begin looking. Katie pulled out a chair and grabbed a pencil and a sheet of paper. Pulling the Pear of Anguish closer, she began to sketch it. The others in the room stopped to watch. Finally getting the basic shape down, Katie began to fill in the intricate decorative detail, which was repeated on all of the pieces. Suddenly her hand stilled. "That's it," she said. Looking up into blank faces, she laid the paper down and in the corner drew an O then put a T through it at a forty-five degree angle. "The design is his initials over and over again along the edges of each piece. From the spacing, I think he has a stencil with four of the symbols which he presses in the hot metal then leaves a space and sets the next set of four."

Everyone acknowledged that they saw the similarity, but it was Michael who said, "We need to find something else with this signature that we can tie to him. Otherwise this could be contested by a defense attorney."

Katie assigned Lucy and Andy to begin searching Tim Owens's online presence. Any social media, any other items from the horse farm that might be public knowledge about the brother's signatures on their pieces, etc. She sent the chief and Tom to the horse farm to talk to Owen and Linder Owens. She and Michael headed to R&R Construction to see if they could locate the job site that Tim was working on.

It took them thirty minutes to find out that Tim hadn't show up for work that morning. They both wanted to head straight to his house, but Michael's coolheaded approach took over. He checked in with the chief and discovered that he and his deputy were on their way back to the station with news. The four of them joined Andy and Lucy, who had taken up residence in the conference room of the police station. Once they were all there, Tom Fuller placed several pieces of decorated metal on the table. All were adorned with the four-pattern symbol found on the ones in the lair.

"Linder confirmed that they were Tim's marks. He said Tim had been out recently using the kiln but he wouldn't say what he was making. Linder knew it wasn't for horses, he had never seen anything shaped like that used on a horse. That's not all. The flower symbol we found on the heads of the screws isn't a flower. It is a central O representing the father with four intersecting O's that look like pedals. It's sort of been the family crest since Owen had all his children." Tom's report was clear and concise, not adding any embellishment or leaving anything out.

Andy spoke up. "We found that symbol on the family's website. Apparently he used to use a larger version to stamp once on the inside of whatever he was making. There isn't anything to indicate when or why he transitioned to the four-pattern symbol."

Katie next told them that Tim had not reported for work and asked Chief Davidson to get an arrest warrant for him. The chief left the conference and went to his office to get started. It took two hours, but finally the warrant came through and the four agents headed out with the chief and five officers.

"Remember, everyone," Chief Davidson said, "Tim is an experienced hunter and there are likely weapons in that house. I don't want any casualties today. Let's be careful." As they all pulled on Kevlar vests and surrounded the house, the chief pulled out his cell phone and dialed Tim's number. The house phone was being monitored and recorded.

Tim answered on the third ring.

"Tim, we have your house surrounded. We know what you did. Now, I don't want anyone getting hurt, so why don't you just come out here and let us have a chat?"

"I wondered how long it would take you to figure out it was me. Once you found the tunnel, I knew it would only be a matter of time." Tim's voice was slurred and thick. He had been drinking for a while. "Those bitches deserved more than what they got. I didn't get to finish cleansing the last two. They were liars as well as the other stuff they did. Barbie pretending to die on me, HOW DARE SHE!" he roared through the phone. "They are all as evil as my Lily. Pretending to love me but sleeping with someone else the whole time. You know, after she died, I couldn't even look at those kids. Who knows if they were even mine. God punished her for me. But he gave me the power to give justice to others. No, Chief, I ain't coming out there. I ain't done nothing wrong. But I'm tired of living like this. There is too much evil in this world." The phone line stayed open as everyone heard the unmistakable sound of a gun discharging.

The agents threw a stun grenade through the window and breached the door. Inside, they found the body of Tim Owens, still clutching his glass of moonshine in one hand and his pistol in the other. The only thing odd about the sight was that the top half of his head was missing.

EPILOGUE

The following Saturday, Katie drove herself to Billy Sheppard's house. He was once again sitting on the porch stringing beans. She got the batch of chocolate chip cookies from the passenger seat, the ones she made using her mother's special recipe, and approached the house. Billy looked up, and once again his hand froze in motion.

"I brought you some cookies, Billy. I thought we could have an informal, off-the-record chat." Katie sat the cookies down beside him.

"I don't know what you're talking about, girl." But his hand reached into the tin of cookies. As he took the first bite, he sighed and closed his eyes. "I haven't had these in nearly thirty years. Never could figure out what your momma did to alter the recipe." Suddenly, his eyes snapped open and met the green-eyed gaze that was so like his cousin Charlene's.

Katie's steel voice said, "Why don't you start at the beginning, Cousin Billy?"

About the Author

Julie is a native of Central Kentucky. After receiving her degree in English, she chose a career in higher education finance. Fifteen years later, she decided to allow her inner creative genius loose and began writing. She has been an avid reader her entire life, with a special love for mysteries, so she thought it fitting to make her first novel one of suspense. Growing up as an Army brat, she has lived in several states and foreign countries. To this day, she enjoys traveling to new places and experiencing new cultures. When at home she is likely to be found enjoying a few extreme sports, such as: rock climbing, scuba diving, or whitewater rafting. Her willingness to enter into activities of mortal peril is balanced by her commitment to ensure the quality of life for animals through her service with various dog rescue organizations. She now lives in Middle Tennessee with her three dogs, Ginny, Holly and Luna.

You can find more at: http://juliemellon.com
Or you can follow her at:
https://www.facebook.com/jlmellonauthor

Printed in Poland
by Amazon Fulfillment
Poland Sp. z o.o., Wrocław